'Alessandro, I ca[n]
it would be a total disaster. People don't get married because they're pregnant.'

'They do. Every day of the week.'

'Well, I don't. The only reason I'd get married is if I was in love with a man.'

His expression like granite, his dark eyes locked onto hers. 'And you don't love me...' His shrug suggested to Sam that he was indifferent to the fact. 'Well, that may be so, but the man you love is not the father of your baby...' A nerve clenched in his lean cheek as he added. 'I am. You will marry me,' he said, fastening the buttons on his shirt. 'When you see sense you know where to find me.' Striding to the door, his back stiff and unyielding, he didn't look back once.

Kim Lawrence comes from English/Irish stock. Though lacking much authentic Welsh blood, she was born and brought up in North Wales. She returned there when she married, and her sons were both born on Anglesey, an island off the coast. Though not isolated, Anglesey is a little off the beaten track, but lively Dublin, which Kim loves, is only a short ferry ride away. Today they live on the farm her husband was brought up on. Welsh is the first language of many people in this area and Kim's husband and sons are all bilingual—she is having a lot of fun, not to mention a few headaches, trying to learn the language!

With small children, the unsocial hours of nursing didn't look attractive. So, encouraged by a husband who thinks she can do anything she sets her mind to, Kim tried her hand at writing. Always a keen Mills & Boon® reader, it seemed natural for her to write a romance novel—now she can't imagine doing anything else. She is a keen gardener and cook, and enjoys running—often on the beach as, living on an island, the sea is never very far away. She is usually accompanied by her Jack Russell, Sprout—don't ask. It's a long story!

THE ITALIAN'S WEDDING ULTIMATUM

BY
KIM LAWRENCE

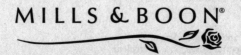

All the characters in this book have no existence outside the imagination of the author, and have no relation whatsoever to anyone bearing the same name or names. They are not even distantly inspired by any individual known or unknown to the author, and all the incidents are pure invention.

First published in Great Britain 2006
Harlequin Mills & Boon Limited,
Eton House, 18-24 Paradise Road, Richmond, Surrey TW9 1SR

© Kim Lawrence 2006

ISBN 0 263 84813 2

Set in Times Roman 10½ on 11¾ pt.
01-0506-54686

Printed and bound in Spain
by Litografia Rosés, S.A., Barcelona

CHAPTER ONE

SAM identified the person who had come to stand behind her chair long before his hands came to rest lightly on her shoulders. Her heart rate quickened a little before she forced herself to relax. As she turned her head her smile stayed in place. It wasn't easy, but Sam had reached the point where she felt pretty well qualified to give a master class in hiding her true feelings.

She firmly steered her thoughts from the self-pitying direction they were drifting. Reality check, Samantha Maguire—you weren't singled out for any particular cruelty from fate. Hearts get broken most days of the week!

So live with it, girl, she told herself sternly.

She was living; in fact she was living *proof* that there was life after a broken heart! Not that she was ever in danger of downplaying the disaster that was unrequited love—when the only person you had ever imagined spending the rest of your life with married someone else you didn't become indifferent overnight, or even after two years. But you did develop a protective shell; you had to.

There were days now when Sam could go an entire morning without thinking about Jonny Trelevan. Admittedly on those occasions she hadn't had a glass of champagne and he didn't have his hand on her shoulder!

Sam suspected that getting on with her life and not brooding on what might have been would probably have been easier if she could have erased him from her life, but that had never been a serious option. There were just too many connections. Not only were the Trelevan and Maguire families friends and neighbours in the small Cornish seaside town where she had been born and brought up, but Jonny's twin, Emma, was one of her best friends. And now, after the christening that morning, they were both godparents to Emma's first daughter, Laurie.

'So this is where you've been hiding, Sam.' Jonny bent down and his lips brushed gently against her cheek.

She was surprised by the unexpected gesture. Jonny wasn't normally a wildly tactile person—at least not with her—and, for a brief moment unable to shield her feelings, Sam dropped her chin and fixed her attention on the baby in her lap while she fought to regain her composure.

Her god-daughter looked back at her and gave a gummy smile. Sam felt a stab of wistful envy for the childlike innocence.

Why are you worrying? she asked herself as she grinned back at the baby and tweaked her button nose. 'Are you laughing at silly Aunty Sam…?' *See—even a ten-month-old knows Jonny wouldn't notice if you stripped naked.*

Or if he did it would only be to ask if she was warm enough! The bottom line was that to Jonny she was always going to be good old Sam—the slightly odd, skinny redhead from next door.

As she lifted her chin a moment later, her serene just-good-friends smile firmly pinned in place, Sam's unwary gaze connected head-on with the enigmatic hooded stare of Alessandro Di Livio, who was standing a little apart from a laughing group of guests on the other side of the room.

She stiffened, and her smile guttered.

A *little apart* just about described the man who, in Sam's opinion, carried 'aloof' to the point of plain rudeness.

With some men she might have suspected that the entire

dark, brooding man-of-mystery thing was cultivated for effect, just to make people notice him. But Alessandro Di Livio didn't need to make the effort.

He got noticed!

Of course he got noticed. He was tall, lean, and rampantly male, and if his body looked *half* as good without clothes as it did—Sam lost the thread momentarily as she thought about him naked. Face rosily tinged, she reined in her wayward imagination and concentrated on his face. Individually, his strong, dark features were memorable; collectively, they were nothing short of perfect. And that was before you even touched on the subject of the forcefield of raw sexuality that preceded him into any room!

Even from this distance the unnerving intensity of his stare had her stomach muscles behaving unpredictably. Without dropping her eyes she rested her chin on the top of the baby's silky head; his eyes really *were* the darkest she had ever seen—not dark warm, but dark *hard*. That man, she thought, repressing a shudder, wasn't chocolate. Not even the dark, bitter variety. He was cold, hard steel!

Despite the familiar wave of antipathy she always experienced when around the Italian financier, Sam forced her lips into a polite smile—while thinking, God, but there's just something about you that sets my teeth on edge.

Actually, not something, she admitted. *Everything!*

From the way he walked into a room as if he owned it to the ability of his deep voice with its tactile quality and intriguing accent to make her skin prickle. Even the fact that his incredibly well-cut suit didn't have a crease in it got under her skin. She knew it was totally irrational, and it probably made her a freak, considering that just about every other female she had ever met drooled when his name was mentioned, but she found his brand of arrogance and raw, in-your-face sexuality a total turn-off.

When she had said as much to Emma, during Jonny and

Kat's belated wedding party, her best friend, who had a pretty warped sense of humour, had grinned slyly and suggested innocently that maybe all this hostility was because Sam was secretly attracted to the Italian.

Well aware that if she showed how repugnant she found the joking suggestion Emma was going to take the *she protests too much* route, she had rolled her eyes and joked, 'Sure I am—I dream about him every night.' Trying not to think about that one shameful occasion she had almost successfully blanked from her mind—the one when she had woken with her entire body bathed in sweat and her heart pumping so fast she'd felt as if she was choking.

Fortunately a girl couldn't be held accountable for what her subconscious got up to.

'I think we'll make a lovely couple,' she'd added.

Disregarding the irony heavily lacing this prognosis, Emma grinned. 'So, you think you're the woman to get our famously commitment-phobic Italian stud to the altar? You do realise that the only time his name has ever been linked with marriage was with that woman…the lawyer…messy divorce, husband a junior minister or something.' Her smooth brow furrowed as she failed to retrieve the name. 'What was her name…?'

'Marisa Sinclair.' When the ring everyone had expected to see appear on her finger hadn't materialised Marisa Sinclair had responded to prying questions by saying that Alessandro was and always would be one of the most important people in her life.

'That's the one. Stunning-looking—half-Scottish, half-Italian, and super smart. But she didn't get her man in the end. You fancy taking a shot, Sam…?'

'You don't think I'm his type?'

Emma ran a mock critical eye over her friend. 'You scrub up pretty well when you make the effort, Sam, but…'

Sam held up a hand. 'I'm no Marisa Sinclair. All right, stop right there, while I still have some self-esteem left,' she pleaded.

'Don't fret, Sam. You're too deep for him. I think he goes for superficial and obvious. You want to know what my theory is about our enigmatic Italian?' Taking Sam's silence as assent—wrongly, as it happened—she went on to explain. 'When they were handing out the pheremones he got a treble dose. Have you seen the way women act when he walks into a room? Honest to God, an expert in body language would have a field-day!'

Thinking about the uncomfortable all over tingle she had personal experience of, Sam nodded.

'All that and money too.' Emma sighed. 'They do say that the *palazzo* on his Tuscan estate is out of this world—though I don't see how anyone knows, because nobody ever gets to go there except a few really close friends.'

'I'm surprised he has any.'

From Emma's amused expression Sam could tell that there were more comments about hostility masking attraction heading her way, so she added quickly. 'Well, maybe now you're related you'll get to see it in person.'

'I hope so. I could do with a couple of weeks in Tuscany this summer. However, if my brother's connections don't get me an invite, I'll just have to rely on my best friend to remember when she lands her dream man.'

Nightmare man, Sam thought, maintaining a long-suffering, smiling silence as her friend dissolved into fits of helpless laughter once more.

Sam sighed and pushed aside the recollections as across the room the man who had been the subject of that long-ago conversation carried on staring, with that same unnerving intensity.

Damn the man, she fumed. He has no manners at all!

It was childish, she knew, and maybe the challenge she thought she read in his eyes was all in her imagination, but

Sam was determined that she wasn't going to be the one to look away first. Consciously allowing her own smile to fade, because making an effort to be polite was clearly wasted on him, she picked up her glass of orange juice and raised it to him in a mocking salute.

The defiant gesture fell rather flat when he didn't respond. His enigmatic dark eyes, with their heavy fringe of curling lashes, just continued to drill into her from across the room.

Sam's resolve was wilting fast, but she was saved a humiliating climb-down when an attractive blonde sidled up to him…sidled so close that her breasts were almost touching his chest. Actually, they *were* touching.

Sam recognised the blonde, who had come with one of Emma's cousins. The girl had been stalking Alessandro with single-minded determination all day. Sam saw her catch hold of his sleeve and thought viciously, Serve you right! It wasn't until he turned his head away that she realised she had been literally holding her breath.

Gasping a little, to draw air into her oxygen-deprived lungs, she put her glass down on a table. What a conceited bore the man is, she thought, her lips thinning contemptuously.

A conceited bore with the ability to make your hands shake just by looking at you.

The warm fingers on her shoulder tightened and Sam's eyes widened. It was kind of shocking to realise that, far from struggling to keep a lid on her feelings for Jonny, she had forgotten he was there! And it was utterly irrational—considering he was not only another woman's husband, but oblivious to the fact she adored him—that Sam felt a pang of guilt.

As if I've been unfaithful! Now, how crazy is that?

'And how are you, my gorgeous one?'

Sam relaxed a little and felt wistful. Jonny's voice was exactly like him. Warm, solid, uncomplicated and reliable. Everything, in fact, that the Italian was not, she thought, unable to repress a tiny shudder as an image of those dark, lean, impossibly symmetrical features formed in her head.

Feeling irritated with herself for allowing Alessandro Di Livio to intrude once more into her thoughts, she angled a warm smile at Jonny. And of course she hadn't for a second made the mistake of thinking that his crooning question had been addressed to *her*.

She'd known it never would be.

It hadn't always been that way, and it was deeply embarrassing to recall that for a long time she had firmly believed that one day the scales would fall from Jonny's eyes and he would finally realise that little Sam Maguire was the only woman he could love.

A rich fantasy life was one thing, Sam mused, but her fantasy had become so firmly embedded that she had believed totally that it was going to happen—to the extent where it had affected the decisions she'd made. This belief had persisted right up to the moment Jonny had arrived home with a stunning girl whom he had proudly introduced to his family as 'my wife.'

'She's pretty much perfect,' Jonny observed now, awkwardly stroking the smooth cheek of his baby niece with a finger.

Much like yourself.

Sam guiltily lowered her eyes and turned her attention back to the baby on her lap, who gave a contented gurgle and captured the pendant around Sam's slim neck.

'She looks just like Emma, doesn't she?'

'Kat thinks she looks like me,' Jonny mused.

'The same thing, really,' Sam pointed out.

The twins, though poles apart personality-wise, had always been very alike in looks. And now that Jonny had given up surfing competitively to run first one and then several more stores across the country selling surf gear, his sun-bleached blond hair had darkened to the same honey-brown as his sister's, so the likeness between the siblings was even more pronounced.

'What's up, Sam…?'

'Up?'

'You sound… I don't know…' He studied her profile. 'Cranky,' he decided.

'I was just thinking about your brother-in-law.'

'Alessandro!' Jonny's eyes automatically sought out the tall figure standing across the room. Their eyes connected and Jonny smiled tensely before looking away. He never had been able to rid himself of the feeling that the older man could read his mind…always an uncomfortable experience, but with the cheque burning a hole in his pocket at that moment particularly so.

She nodded. 'He may have a perfect face, but his manners could do with some major work.' Seeing Jonny's brows lift at the spitting vehemence of her declaration, Sam cautioned herself to downplay her dislike. 'You have to admit,' she challenged in a milder tone, 'he makes no effort whatsoever.'

'Effort to do what?'

She pursed her lips into a disapproving line. 'Mingle.'

'Mingle!' Jonny echoed, and laughed.

'He always gives the impression that he's looking down his nose at me…at everyone…but then I suppose he thinks he doesn't need to be polite to ordinary people like us,' she observed contemptuously.

Jonny gave a shrug, still looking amused. 'Oh, you know Alessandro.'

For once Sam found Jonny's laid-back attitude irritating. 'Happily, no, I don't. We don't exactly move in the same circles.'

'He's actually a pretty private person, Sam, and with the paparazzi on his case all the time, sniffing for a scandal, you can't really blame him for being a bit cautious.'

'He's not cautious. He's stuck up and snobbish. Still, at least he's safe from the paparazzi today.' Nobody was going to expect to see Alessandro Di Livio at a christening in a Cornish seaside village.

Jonny looked at her curiously. 'God, you really don't like him, do you, Sam?'

'He doesn't like me,' she countered.

Jonny looked startled by the suggestion. 'Oh, I doubt that.' His eyes moved from her bright copper head and slid over her trim but slight figure. 'He's probably not even noticed you, Sam.'

From his expression it was obvious that Jonny thought she'd be pleased to realise that she was actually too insignificant even to register on Alessandro Di Livio's radar.

Sam forced a smile. 'You mean I'm mistaking indifference for rudeness?'

The ironic inflection in her voice sailed over Jonny's head. 'He can be a bit stand-offish,' he admitted. 'And he's not a great talker—at least not with me. But then he still thinks I'm not good enough for Kat.' He lowered his voice and recalled, 'You know, the night we told him we'd got married I was expecting an explosion, but the guy didn't turn a hair. Then later, when Kat wasn't in the room, he told me that if I ever hurt her he would make me wish I'd never been born.' The recollection made him shudder.

'He threatened you?' Sam bristled with indignation. The man was nothing but a thug!

'It was more in the nature of a promise.'

'I hope you told him where he could put his threats.'

Jonny looked amused. 'Yeah, that's *really* likely.'

'You have to stand up to bullies,' Sam contended angrily.

'He wasn't being a bully, he was looking out for his sister—and I don't really blame him. He's been fine with me since, but I've never forgotten, and he...' Jonny shrugged. 'Alessandro doesn't forget anything,' he admitted.

'Well, I think you and Kat were made for each other!' Sam declared, meaning it.

It *should* have been easy to dislike Kat. She had it all—pots of money, beauty and Jonny. But it wasn't! It was impossible not to like Jonny's wife, who was as warm, spontaneous and sweet-natured as her brother was revolting, cold and conceited.

'But he's right.' Jonny sighed gloomily. 'I'm not good enough for her.'

'Rubbish. Since when is Alessandro Di Livio the expert on relationships? The only person he's likely to form a loving and long relationship with is his own reflection!'

Jonny chuckled. 'Don't let Kat hear you say that,' he warned, flashing a guilty look towards his wife. 'As far as she is concerned, Alessandro can do no wrong. But then,' he added, a note of defence creeping into his voice, 'he did virtually bring her up single-handed after their parents were killed in that crash.'

Sam felt a cold shiver running down her spine and gave the baby a sudden hug, closing her eyes and burying her face deeper in the comforting warmth of her sweet-smelling soft hair.

The crash Jonny referred to had killed two members of the famous aristocratic Italian family and left a third fighting for his life. It must have had saturation media coverage at the time, but Sam, who had only been in her teens, had only a vague recollection of the story. Coincidentally, she had caught a TV programme only the previous night, in which it had featured prominently.

In asking *Are Some People Born Lucky?*, the programme-makers had presented a pretty compelling argument that some people *did* lead a charmed existence, surviving situations which logically they should not have.

The programme had made compulsive viewing, but it had had the sort of voyeuristic qualities that made Sam feel uncomfortable. She had been about to vote with her feet and switch off when a computer simulation had shown the route the Di Livio car had taken when it had gone over the cliff-edge, and she had literally held her breath as she watched the action replay.

Sam hadn't been surprised to hear emergency workers

comment that it had been the first time they had ever taken anyone out of a wreck alive on that treacherous mountainside.

When the commentator's voice had posed in thrilling accents the question 'Was this man born lucky?' the screen had been filled with the image of a young-looking Alessandro, his dark hair whitened with dust, his bruised face leeched of all colour, strapped to a stretcher about to be air lifted away from the twisted, mangled remains of the car.

Sam had then switched off the TV and muttered angrily to the cat, '*Lucky?* Very lucky, if your version of lucky happens to involve nearly dying and losing both your parents… *Idiots!*'

She had caught sight of her scowling reflection in the mirror and stopped dead, her eyes widening. I'm getting all protective and indignant on behalf of Alessandro Di Livio…now, how bizarre is that? One thing was for sure, she'd thought, flashing a wry smile at her mirror image. The recipient of her caring concern would not have been grateful!

The programme had preyed on her mind. She just hadn't been able to get the image of his tragic, blood-stained face out of her head, no matter how hard she'd tried. Then this morning at the church, as she'd sat alone and waited for everyone else to arrive, in he'd walked!

It had really spooked her—think about him and he appears… That will teach me to be more careful about who and what I think about in the future, she had reflected, shrinking back into her seat.

Unobserved, she'd had the luxury of being able to stare at him. People would probably pay for that privilege. But, no matter how hard she'd looked, she hadn't found any trace of the vulnerability she had seen in the face of that young man with the bleak, empty eyes, clinging to life.

Same classical profile, same aquiline nose, same razor-sharp prominent cheekbones, and his mouth was still sexy enough to cause a sharp intake of breath in the unprepared observer, but the man exuded an air of unstudied confidence and control.

If she had glimpsed even a shadow of that younger man Sam thought her attitude to him might have softened, but she hadn't, and when a few moments later she'd knocked a hymn book to the floor and alerted him to her presence she had looked away quickly.

'I saw a programme about the accident last night,' she said now.

Jonny nodded. 'Yeah, Alessandro phoned Kat and told her not to watch it. He said it was sensationalist rubbish and would only upset her.'

'And did she watch it?'

'After he'd told her not to?' Jonny laughed at the notion of Kat not following her brother's suggestion.

'Well, he may be a control freak, but in this instance,' Sam admitted, 'he was right. It *would* have upset her. It was a bit graphic.' A chilly shiver traced a path down her spine as she recalled the bleak devastation in the eyes of the man they had called lucky.

'I suppose he's afraid it will resurrect the story.'

'How old was Kat at the time?' Jonny's wife had only been nineteen when they'd married, after a whirlwind romance.

'She was eleven. She would have been with them on the trip, but she spiked a fever at the last minute…turned out she had mumps.'

'Lucky mumps,' Sam said thinking about the moment that morning in church, when her eyes had brushed Alessandro's. Her smooth brow furrowed. Jonny's wrong. He *doesn't* like me. Her chin came up to a belligerent angle.

Which suits me fine!

Her grim expression lightened as Laurie's fingers closed over the beaten silver pendant she wore around her neck and she tried to draw it to her rosebud mouth. Sam, grateful to be distracted from her thoughts, disentangled the tenacious chubby fingers and shook her head.

'No, Laurie, it wouldn't taste good,' she reproached.

Jonny's fingers tightened on her shoulder. 'Feeling broody, Sam?'

The question sounded teasing and light, but something in his voice made Sam lift her head and study his face. '*Broody—me*…?' Jonny smiled, but she noticed it didn't reach his eyes. 'I prefer babies when you can hand them back at the end of the day.' Not true, but it sounded like a suitable response. She could hardly go with the other option, which was to say *If I can't have your babies I don't want any!*

'You think that now, but all women start talking babies.'

Sam received a jolt as his meaning sank in. Jonny a father… It would happen one day, so get used to it. 'Are congratulations in order?'

Jonny didn't respond to her question. Following the direction of his distracted gaze, Sam saw his eyes had come to rest on Kat.

Feeling like an intruder, Sam quickly averted her gaze, trying and failing to imagine a man looking at *her* with the kind of suppressed longing she had read in Jonny's face. She caught a glimpse of herself reflected in the enormous gilt-framed mirror that covered the wall to her right and thought, *Sure—that's really going to happen.* It was a fact of life that freckles, red hair and a body that was never going to be curvy did not inspire dumbstruck lust and longing.

'Congratulations?' Jonny dragged his attention back to Sam. 'I thought you and Kat might be starting a family.'

Her innocuous remark caused Jonny's good-looking features to freeze. 'I'm not ready to start a family.'

Meaning Kat was…? Sam speculated, puzzling over his expression. 'I thought you loved children…'

Not that she could for a second imagine Jonny as a hands-on father. Though he had many good points, Jonny did have some pretty old-fashioned ideas.

'This isn't a good time.'

'Is there ever a good time?'

Dark colour flooded Jonny's face as he bent closer. 'For God's sake, Sam,' he hissed. 'Do I have to spell it out? You of all people should realise that I can't *afford* to be thinking of babies. And I can't tell Kat…' He swallowed, drew a deep breath and shook his head. The strained smile he gave her was ruefully apologetic. 'Sorry, Sam. I shouldn't take it out on you.' Absently he patted her shoulder. 'Could I have a word, Sam?'

He looked so apologetic that she immediately forgave his outburst. 'Isn't that what we *are* doing?'

Jonny cleared his throat and nodded towards the closed French doors. '*In private.*'

You can have anything you want.

Her colour slightly heightened by her traitorous thought, Sam nodded placidly and reminded herself for the tenth time that afternoon that she was a strong, independent woman who didn't need a man—and, anyway, she wasn't the sort of person who would settle for second best.

In the alcove, where he had retreated to watch them, Alessandro Di Livio tightened his long fingers around the stem of his untouched glass of champagne as he observed his brother-in-law's head move closer to the glossy copper one of the seated woman.

They were so close they looked like lovers about to embrace. He couldn't give the man his sister had chosen a backbone, but he could make damned sure that he didn't cheat and break his besotted little sister's heart!

God knew what either woman saw in him. Maybe it was the surfing thing? He presumed, from the cabinet of trophies ostentatiously on show in his sister's apartment, that the younger man had been more successful riding the waves than he was at business. Perhaps the younger man could have coped with one store, he conceded, but his rapid and reckless expansion over the past eighteen months had been nothing short of suicidal. The only thing that surprised Alessandro, who had been set to bail him out for the past year, was that he was still financially afloat.

His sensually sculpted lips formed a twisted, cynical smile as the Maguire woman lifted her hand in a fluttery gesture to her slender, pale throat. The action was as revealing as he had come to expect of her, but he couldn't quite decide if she was as transparent as she appeared, or if it was all part of some sort of act.

Alessandro's nostrils flared. If Jonny Trelevan didn't know she was his for the asking the younger man was an even bigger fool than he'd taken him for. His eyes slid towards his sister, who had been talking too loudly and brightly all afternoon, and found she too was watching the couple. As he watched she turned her head, and he was sure he caught the glitter of tears in her eyes.

Whatever was wrong with his sister's marriage, he would have laid odds that the red-headed little witch was responsible. What was her game? Alessandro wondered as he angled his dark head a little to one side and studied the slim figure.

If asked to classify her look he would have called it sexy, yet demure. Not to his taste, but he knew a lot of men went for the perennial virgin look. She was the sort of female who simultaneously aroused predatory and protective instincts in the opposite sex.

No wonder men got confused around her. They didn't know whether to kiss her or protect her from a light breeze! He, on the other hand, knew what he wanted to do—namely shake her and tell her to display a little more discretion when she looked at Trelevan with those big hungry eyes!

Of course her dress sense was nothing short of a total disaster, but colour co-ordination wasn't going to be high on your average male's list of priorities when he heard her laugh—that low, husky, wicked chuckle.

It was the sort of laugh a man imagined hearing behind a closed bedroom door. *Or is that just me…?*

He had known from the beginning, of course, that she was in love with Jonny Trelevan—though astonishingly, as far as he could tell, he was the only person who did! Her friends and relations seemed uniformly oblivious to the intense misery behind the brave smile. He had suspected at that time that if you had taken away that smile and the screaming tension in every fibre of her slender body she would probably have collapsed.

He was neither a relation or a friend, but an objective observer, so her unrequited love was none of his concern so long as she represented no danger to his sister's happiness.

He had decided to give her the benefit of the doubt.

For starters, Trelevan had seemed to view her as one of the boys, and the only time he got physical was when he punched her playfully on the arm.

As for the girl herself… His eyes narrowed as once again they fell on Samantha Maguire, face buried in the hair of the baby on her lap, so that all he could see was the top of her copper head. If he had thought she represented a threat to his sister's happiness he would have taken whatever action he deemed necessary. But two years ago he had decided that she did not possess the tempestuous nature that was meant to accompany her vibrant colouring.

She would look, but not touch. And there was no law against looking. He had done some of that himself. On every occasion since, when their paths had crossed, he had kept a watchful eye on her.

Of course he'd been glad that Katerina did not have the added complication of a jealous would-be lover in the background, trying to sabotage her marriage, but he'd felt a stab of contempt when he considered the Maguire girl's passive acceptance of the hand fate had dealt her. It was incomprehensible to him, but maybe, he mused, it had something to do with British stoicism—something which Alessandro with his more volatile Latin temperament had never been able to get a handle on. But then he never had understood people taking pride in being a good loser.

Now, though, he wasn't so sure about his earlier assessment. Had he been mistaken in her? Had Samantha Maguire been playing the long game and waiting for her chance? Alessandro was not the sort of man who left things to chance, and this was a possibility he had to consider.

Jonny Trelevan wasn't the husband he would have chosen for his sister—he was too weak and ineffectual to Alessandro's mind—but Alessandro had accepted that his wishes were not the ones that counted. The younger man was the husband Kat wanted, and as her brother he would do any-thing in his power to give Katerina, deprived of the parental love and support he himself had enjoyed, what she wanted.

He stood listening to the inane prattle of the young woman at his side, catching only one word in three of what she was saying, and plunged headlong into one of the flashbacks which had been part of his life for the last ten years.

CHAPTER TWO

A FLASHBACK implied that you'd lost sense of your surroundings, but for Alessandro it was more a sense of dislocation, of being in two places at the same time.

Like today—in the here and now he was saying something that made the plastic blonde girl giggle, while simultaneously he was back on the dark road of that night, pressing the brakes and feeling no response.

The only outward evidence of what was happening to him was the sheen of sweat across his brow.

He could hear the blonde listing her favourite haunts. The flickering images always followed the same rigid sequence. He knew that the next one involved being pretty sure he was going to die.

'I don't go to nightclubs,' he replied, when she finally asked his own preference.

She could have looked no more shocked had he confided a predilection for women's underwear. Alessandro might have laughed had he not been calling on every skill he had, and then some he didn't, in a futile attempt to control the car. Knowing as he did so that nothing he could do would affect the outcome.

Looking at the card scrawled with a number, he nodded and murmured an ironic, 'You're very kind,' as his guts tightened in anticipation of the car launching itself into space.

Then the blonde was gone, and so was the car, and they

were falling on and on. He could hear the high-pitched female scream that seemed to go on for ever, and then the screech of metal as it ripped and tore. The foul stench of petrol filled his flared nostrils.

Wiping a hand across his damp brow, he looked across the room and saw Samantha Maguire on the point of stepping through the French windows with his brother-in-law. Watching the couple slip outside, Alessandro narrowed his eyes in speculative anger. Did they think nobody had noticed?

Maybe conducting their illicit relationship under the very nose of Katerina added spice? Or maybe the redhead *wanted* to be discovered?

In his head there was silence, an eerie silence broken finally by his own voice calling to his parents, asking, 'Are you all right?'

Imprisoned in his seat, he could only imagine why there was no reply to the question he kept repeating, and all the time he had the knowledge that it would take only one spark and the car and its contents would become a raging inferno.

Dawn had been breaking before the first rescuers had arrived.

Alessandro had still been in hospital when the inquest was held. And, thanks to the irritating intransigence of the surgeon responsible for uniting the shattered fragments of bone in his right leg, he had been banned from attending.

His personality was such that going against expert opinion did not normally present him with an obstacle. Alessandro's problem on that occasion was that the expert advice he wanted to flout came from the man who had saved his leg when the general consensus of medical opinion had been that the mangled limb was beyond saving. He figured that following his advice was the least he owed the man who had operated not once but three times to give him back his mobility.

The inquest had gone ahead in his absence, and had resulted in the total recall of a series of high-performance cars, all of which had shared the faulty braking system discovered in the one that had plunged off the side of the mountain with him at the wheel. The fact that no blame for the fatal accident had been assigned to him personally, that in fact the crash investigators had said nothing he could have done would have prevented the car going over, did not lessen the responsibility that Alessandro felt for the death of his parents.

He had relived the disastrous moments innumerable times since, sure that if he had done something differently his parents would still be alive. Not that it was in his nature to waste time indulging his survivor guilt. He'd had a sister to bring up—a sister who, thanks to him, had no parents.

His chiselled jaw tightened as, without waiting for his heart-rate to return to normal, he made his way towards the terrace doors. The expression on his face made several people get out of his way.

It was time to issue a warning—a warning that was long overdue. And if Miss Maguire knew what was good for her she would take notice. If not? Well, that was her decision. For his part, Alessandro had no doubts concerning his ability to make her see things his way.

The terrace was empty because, despite the brilliant April sunshine, the fluffy white clouds and the expanse of daffodils on the wide green lawns, the wind held a bone-biting chill.

Sam shivered as the wind cut through the beige linen suit she wore. The skirt length and A-line cut didn't do her petite, narrow-hipped and high-bosomed frame any favours. As her mother had pointed out earlier, she should never, *ever* wear beige as it made her look drained and haggard.

Sam had agreed. And of course since then she had *felt* drained and haggard.

'God, I'm going to get hypothermia,' she said, hugging her arms around herself as a particularly harsh gust of wind cut through the fabric. 'Couldn't you say what you needed to say inside?'

'Here.'

Sam looked from the envelope he had thrust into her hand to Jonny's solemn face. 'What's this?' she asked, making no attempt to open it. She knew what it was.

He ran a hand through his disordered fair curls, and the familiar gesture made Sam's heart ache. 'I said I'd repay the loan, Sam,' he reminded her.

'And I said there was no hurry, Jonny,' she returned quietly, hating the way his eyes slid from hers. 'I don't need the money. It's just sitting there in the bank.' The amount of money that worldwide sales of the *Angela's Cat* series made was shockingly large, and Sam's tastes were pretty simple. And in a funny way she owed her success to Jonny.

Without Jonny she would never have felt the need to escape, and she might never have discovered that writing was the perfect way to do so. In which case the chances were her children's story might never have been anything more than a few pages lying forgotten in the back of a drawer. And she might still be working as a supply teacher.

'You helped me out of a sticky spot, and for that, Sam, I'll be eternally grateful. But,' he said, closing her fingers around the envelope, 'this is yours. And thanks to you Kat isn't going to know how close to bankrupt I was.'

Sam gave a worried frown and hoped Jonny's male pride wasn't making him repay the loan before he could afford to. But, aware she couldn't do much about it, she reluctantly shoved the envelope into her pocket. 'Well, you know what I think, Jonny.'

'That I should have told Kat I was on the verge of bankruptcy.' He shook his fair head and gave a grim laugh. 'Leave it, Sam. You don't know what you're talking about. I *had* to borrow that money.'

'But your grandmother's legacy—' Sam protested.

'Paid for the initial investment,' he slotted in. 'And I needed money to expand.'

'Why expand?'

Jonny's features settled into obstinate lines. 'I couldn't expect Kat to be a shopkeeper's wife.'

Sam shook her head in exasperation. 'For the record, I think you're a total idiot. Your wife is rich, and her brother is—'

Jonny ran an unsteady hand over his cleanshaven jaw and interrupted. 'Her brother is *Alessandro Di Livio*. That's the whole point, Sam. He's worth billions, and I—'

'Kat knew you weren't a billionaire when she married you,' she interrupted impatiently.

His blue eyes slid from hers. 'How could I tell a girl like Kat that I was taking less out of the shop in a year than she spends on shoes in a month? Her brother has always given her everything she wants before she even asks. She worships him,' he gritted, unable to conceal the envy in his voice as he added dourly, 'And, let's face it, Alessandro is perfect.'

An image of a dark, patrician face flashed into her head, and Sam was unable to voice the denial she would have liked. Physically at least he was about as close to perfect as you could get. If your idea of perfect happened to be six feet five of lean, toned muscle, flashing dark eyes, a sinfully sensual mouth, cheekbones that you could cut yourself on and an aristocratic profile. His gorgeous Mediterranean colouring presumably went all over…

She stopped, alarm filtering into her expression. Mentally undressing the man twice within the space of half an hour was not a good development.

Well, gorgeous body or not, he wasn't Sam's idea of perfect. But she accepted that on this she was in the minority. However, it didn't take a great leap to see how a creature like that could make other men feel inadequate.

'Tell me, Jonny, what's the most important thing in your life?' she asked him quietly.

'Kat, of course.'

Sam heard the indignation in his voice that she should need to ask, and wondered bleakly if the other woman knew how lucky she was. 'Exactly.' Her lips twitched into a contemptuous smile. 'Can you imagine a woman being the most important thing in Alessandro Di Livio's life?'

She watched Jonny struggle to do so, and gave a triumphant *I told you so* smile. 'Of course you can't. Because the only person important to Alessandro Di Livio is Alessandro.'

'He cares about Kat!' Jonny protested.

Too much, Sam thought. 'Fair enough,' she conceded. 'But if Kat had wanted another version of her brother she'd have found one. She didn't, because she's a hell of a lot brighter than you are. What she wanted was a decent bloke who puts her first. She wanted you, Jonny.'

'You really think so?'

'How would you like it if Kat was in trouble and she didn't come to you? Just stop being a stiff-necked idiot, tell your wife the truth, and give her what she wants…which presumably is you, Jonny.' There's a lot of it about, she thought, before adding, 'And maybe a baby…?'

The anger died from Jonny's face and he clutched his head in his hands. 'God, Sam, you're right!' he cried. 'I've been a total idiot. I know I should have told her. But I didn't want her to think she'd married a total loser!'

Sam had got into the habit of avoiding physical contact with Jonny—it was a self-protective thing—but if ever there was an occasion for a hug this was it. 'God,' she said, wrapping her arms around him, 'but men are stupid.'

Jonny, who had rested his chin on her glossy hair, lifted his head. 'Especially me.'

'Especially you,' she agreed with a watery grin as she drew back from the embrace.

'One thing, Sam…?'

'Anything.'

'Don't say anything about this to Alessandro. Like I said, he never did think I was good enough for Kat, and if he found out about my cashflow problems he'd…Well…'

Sam nodded. 'I understand.'

She understood, all right. She understood that the only way Jonny's marriage was going to work out was if Kat managed to escape her brother's overpowering influence.

'My lips are sealed,' she promised, miming a zipping motion along the generous curve of her mouth.

About to turn away, Jonny swung back and took her by the shoulders. 'Sam, I may not say so very often, but I do know that you're the best friend in the world!' he said, planting a light kiss on her lips.

'Sure I am. Now, go and talk to your wife.'

Oblivious to the husky catch in her voice, Jonny responded to her urging, pausing only to blow a kiss back to her from the doorway as he dived back indoors, his expression determined.

Sam forgot her desire to escape the cold wind and closed her eyes, lifting a hand to her lips. Her smooth brow puckered into a frown. No tingling…no wild surge of uncontrollable lust! In fact, no lust at all. Could it be that her under-used sex drive had simply died?

'That was a very *touching* scene.'

CHAPTER THREE

THE air was expelled from her lungs in one startled gasp as Sam spun around, thinking, *It can't be…?*

Of course it was. Nobody else had a voice like that.

'Oh, it's you…' she said stupidly, then flushed.

Alessandro watched as she pushed the strands of hair that had come free from the loose knot on her head from her face with both hands. It was an almost child-like gesture. The vibrant copper, he noticed, glowed against her pale skin. Actually, now that he thought about it, her skin glowed too, with an almost opalescent sheen.

It was the sort of skin a man would find difficult to look at and not think about touching…the silky softness was a tactile invitation. His brother-in-law had clearly decided it was an invitation, he thought, his angular jaw tightening as he looked at the lips the younger man had found so irresistible.

Sam's expression grew defensive as she returned the silent, hostile stare of the person responsible for a tingling that extended to the soles of her feet. Inside her chest her heart was banging against her ribcage like a trapped wild animal.

Actually, her trapped wild animal instincts were kicking in pretty hard right now. It was only the fact that he stood between her and the door that stopped her from fleeing.

When she had asked Emma earlier why on *earth* she had invited the wretched man, her friend had reminded Sam that she'd invited all her own family, and he was Kat's brother and she didn't have any other family, poor thing.

'Besides,' she had admitted with a rueful grin, 'I never expected him to actually accept.'

Now, looking up into that lean, arresting face, Sam, who if she was honest had been exasperated by Jonny's inability to stand up for himself where his brother-in-law was concerned, felt a strong surge of sympathy for him. Small wonder he felt nervous and inadequate around the man—and as for confiding his problems…! Dear God, banana skins probably got out of the way when they saw his hand-made Italian shoes coming!

His was certainly the very last shoulder *she'd* choose to cry on, she thought as her glance brushed the broad, well-developed area in question. How many women had made use of those manly shoulders? Or even sunk their teeth into that smooth golden flesh during a moment of heightened passion…?

You didn't look at Alessandro Di Livio and think, Here's a man with empathy. You thought, Here's a man who's never put a foot wrong in his life… *Or a man who inspired women to bite his shoulders?* You thought, Here's a man who has no insight and even less sympathy for the failings of lesser mortals… *And maybe the ability to make a woman lose control…?*

A flurry of alarm filtered into her guarded expression as she wondered where those maverick thoughts had come from.

Had he heard any of her conversation with Jonny?

Her alarm lessened as she realised that unless he'd been lurking in the shadows for a long time, which didn't seem likely, he couldn't know about the cheque burning a hole in her pocket. The most he could have witnessed was a quick hug between friends and a peck on the cheek—so nothing incriminating there.

Sam released a tiny sigh of relief. Jonny's secret was safe.

'I'm sorry—I didn't see you there.' Her normally sunny smile was on the stiff side, but she quietly congratulated herself for making the effort—even though all she wanted to do was escape from his oppressive presence.

'*Obviously.*'

'Is there a problem?'

Considering the degree of hostility emanating from his lean body, it now seemed laughable that on the occasions when Sam had previously encountered the man she had considered him to have a glacially cold disposition. A man with the coldest eyes she had ever seen. A man totally incapable of spontaneous emotion, or for that matter *any* emotion that wasn't clinically calculated.

The nerve jumping erratically alongside his sinfully sexy mouth and the combustible air of barely suppressed fury that was emanating from him now rather suggested that he was capable of doing a lot more than raising his voice. He was certainly raising the hairs on the nape of her neck. She refused point-blank to analyse the things his proximity was doing to any points south of her neck!

His dark eyes meshed with hers. '*You* are the problem.' And one he was going to sort once and for all.

Sam stared, totally bemused by his aggressive response. 'Have you been drinking?'

'No, I have not been drinking. I saw you throw yourself at him.'

Sam shook her head at this harsh addition. 'Throw…? Who…?'

His dark eyes flicked across her slightly parted lips and his own moved in a moue of distaste. 'Kiss him…' He smiled cynically as he watched the guilty colour fly to her pale cheeks. 'There is a name for women who do that to married men.'

This last contemptuous observation and that horrid smile snuffed out the guilt Sam had nursed for the secret she carried in her heart and loosened the firm grip she normally kept on her Celtic redhead's temper. She trembled with the force of the surge of anger that washed over her as she read the superior condemnation in his face.

If she hadn't been in the grip of strong emotions—namely

the desire to physically remove the nasty smile from his smug face—she might have remembered that it probably wasn't a good idea to antagonise someone who was in a position to make Jonny's life uncomfortable. But caution wasn't part of her plan as, head flung back, she took a step towards him.

The sheer, unmitigated nerve of the man—looking down his nose at her like that. Especially when you considered this was the same person who had refused to deny or confirm the rumours that he was the *real* reason a high-profile politician and his lawyer wife had split up. He was obviously as guilty as sin! Sam chose to ignore the fact that at the time she had argued with a friend that silence did not equate to guilt.

'You have something against kissing…?' she asked, injecting sarcasm into her voice and being rewarded by the expression on his face.

Clean up your own act before you criticise other people, she thought grimly.

'Is that kissing generally…?' A finger pressed to the soft indentation in her firmly rounded chin, she pretended to consider this possibility. 'No,' she said, shaking her head from side to side. 'That can't be right. Because you appeared to have nothing against kissing at that film premiere, when that girl was eating your face.' The tasteless pictures had been plastered over every tabloid's front page the next day.

Sam almost laughed. He couldn't have looked more astonished if one of the pieces of furniture had spoken up for itself. She was dimly aware, somewhere in the recesses of her mind, that the adrenaline rush she was experiencing was responsible for half the things coming out of her mouth. Her inability to back down in the face of warning signs you'd have to be blind not to see was down to her own stupidity.

Her breath coming in short, shallow bursts, she studied his proud, patrician features. Hard disdain and anger was implicit in every intriguing hollow and strong plane. His nostrils were flared and his firm jaw tight, and his golden skin was drawn taut across the angles of his jutting cheekbones.

'The lady in question was not married.'

That made a change, then. 'Nor very fussy, it would seem.' She sniffed, and smiled sweetly in response to his hoarsely ejaculated, 'Dio mio!'

'But then some people will endure almost anything to advance their careers. I suppose I'm just lucky that I didn't need to sleep my way to the top.'

Sam registered the dark glitter visible through the mesh of his long lashes and her stomach took a lurching dive. It was only sheer bloody-minded obstinacy—of which her nearest and dearest said she had been gifted an extra portion—that enabled Sam to maintain eye contact.

'You are at the top, then, are you…?' His smile said more clearly than any words that he thought she was lying.

The comment made Sam, normally the most self-deprecating of creatures, who would have been the first to play down her success, stick out her chin and boast boldly, 'I will be.' Her long-suffering editor, who was often heard to despair over her lack of drive and ambition, would have stared to hear that. 'And wherever I am,' she added, with the confidence of someone who knew a company wanted her to write a TV serialisation of the accident-prone feline she had created, 'at least I won't have to rely on my looks to stay there.'

There was a pause as his dark glance moved down her reed-slender figure. 'That is indeed fortunate.' Actually, she had the sort of delicate bone structure that would enable her to grow old gracefully. And lily-pale flawless skin. His eyes slid over the graceful length of her slender neck and the line between his brows deepened.

Two can play at that game, mate, she thought, smiling at him through gritted teeth. 'Nor do I have to worry that people want to be my friend just because of what I can do for them.'

'I consider myself an excellent judge of character.'

Sam's malicious smile widened. In a rather perverse way she was almost enjoying this exchange of smiling insults. Of course she would have enjoyed kicking his shins even more, but as she was no longer six the option wasn't open. 'Of course you do. But this time you have got it so wrong you're going to feel very stupid.'

'I doubt that.'

'Being able to admit when you're wrong is a sign of maturity.'

'A subject *you* would not know one hell of a lot about.'

Great—so now I'm childish, and I go around kissing married men! Sam, who didn't like the way his dark eyes were lingering on her mouth, decided enough was enough—even if the verbal tussle *was* exhilarating. 'Look, you've got it wrong—'

'I know what I saw.'

His sheer bloody-minded intransigence made her want to scream. 'And even if I *did* kiss him, what business would it be of yours?' Even before she saw his expression she knew that he'd interpret her angry retort as an admission of guilt. Frankly, she was past caring.

'Katerina is my sister, and I will protect her.'

She gave up trying to prove her innocence and asked, 'How are you going to stop me sleeping with Jonny?'

'I think telling him you are mine will have the desired effect.'

He said it so matter of factly that Sam thought at first she had misunderstood him. The uncertainty only lasted a moment. There was no room for misinterpretation in his ruthless smile. Honestly, this man belonged in a different century! *Mine,* he had said... As though *owning* someone body and soul was perfectly acceptable.

The idea of surrendering control to a man like Alessandro Di Livio was a concept that made her shudder with horror... *Are you so sure it's horror?*

Sam swallowed. 'I take it you're not an advocate of political correctness?' she observed, moistening her dry lips with her tongue. She inhaled and raised her eyes, only to discover his burning gaze was fixed on her mouth. As their eyes connected the blaze of raw hunger in his nailed her to the spot.

Paralysed by a stab of lust so strong she couldn't breathe, Sam stared up at him. He reminded her of a sleek jungle cat—beautiful, and totally ruthless. She had always considered the claim that danger was attractive a particularly stupid one. Now she knew that she had been very wrong. The fear she had denied feeling moments earlier was now coursing through her veins, along with some primitive stuff she had no intention of *ever* analysing.

There was no point. None of this was real, she told herself. It was all the result of some freak chain of events—events that were *never* going to happen again. She was never going to feel this way again. She was going to go home and close the door and everything would go back to the way it had been before Alessandro Di Livio had looked at her as if he wanted to rip off her clothes.

Sam closed her eyes, thought about closing that door, and felt slightly calmer. She might get a new safety bolt fitted… She opened her eyes and pointed out the obvious flaw in his manipulative plan.

'Jonny wouldn't believe it…' She thought about it, and added. '*Nobody* would believe you.'

'Why not?'

Was he serious? Her eyes travelled up the long, lean, gorgeous length of him before settling on his dark, fallen angel features. 'Because you're…' She just stopped short of saying *incredibly beautiful,* and substituted a husky, 'I don't like you. *Everyone* knows that.'

One dark brow lifted at *everyone,* and he looked amused. 'Liking is not a prerequisite to…' he slotted in.

'Ownership…?' she suggested sweetly. 'Look, this conversation is going nowhere—but *I* am.'

She edged towards the door, but he blocked her way with his body.

Lips pursed and eyes narrowed, she glared up at him. 'You're in my way.'

'Before you go I want to make very sure that you know it would be unwise for you to continue your pursuit of Trelevan.'

A whistling sound of frustration escaped her clenched teeth. My God, the man was fixated! 'Where do you get off, making a judgement about me?' she demanded, indignation making her voice shrill. 'How many times have we met…? Five…? How dare you? You don't even know me!'

'Eight. Not including today.'

The smooth correction made her stare. 'You were counting…?' Her brows lifted and she laughed nervously. 'Should I be flattered?' Her expression hardened. 'Or afraid…? You'd like that, wouldn't you? But then bullies always do,' she contended grimly. 'Only I'm not afraid of you, Mr Di Livio. Not at all,' she stressed shakily, before she was forced to pause to gasp for breath.

'There is nothing preventing us getting to know one another better, if that is what you would like.'

Sam rubbed her damp palms against her skirt and didn't even let herself *think* about what he meant by that. 'Other than mutual dislike. And I *wouldn't* like.'

'Dislike…?' he mused contemplatively. After a moment he shook his dark head and a predatory smile split his lean features. 'Dislike is such a mild word. I think it goes much deeper with us than mere *dislike.*'

The tactile quality she had noticed before in his deep, darkly textured voice was stronger than ever. Sam swallowed. This man really did have the market in enigmatic and disturbing cornered!

'You lack caution and judgement.'

'I was just thinking the same thing.' Her response had worryingly little to do with caution and a lot to do with the excitement that was tying her stomach in knots! 'Now, if you'll excuse me, it's a bit cold out here.' Actually, she no longer felt the cold—her skin was burning.

Instead of moving out of her way, he leaned against the ajar door, causing it to close with a loud click.

Sam's voice was flat, even though inside she was panicking. 'Excuse me…'

His dark eyes slid down her slim figure before returning to her face. The overt contempt in his expression brought a sparkle of anger to Sam's wide-spaced eyes.

'No, I will not excuse you.'

Taken aback by the overt provocation in his response Sam blinked.

A long silence followed, which he showed no signs of filling until he suddenly said accusingly, 'Your eyes have turned green.'

'Pardon me…?' It was possible she had misheard him. It was equally possible her aquamarine eyes *had* turned green. This happened when she was in the grip of strong emotions. Chameleon eyes, her father called them. Though the colour-change did not disguise but reveal the depth of her feelings.

'No, I will not do that either.' Without warning he reached out and took her chin in between long brown fingers and carried on looking into her eyes, which were still green. 'You would not want me for an enemy, *cara.*'

Gazing up into the dark mesmeric depth of his astounding eyes, Sam felt the breath leave her body in one long, shuddering sigh. Her knees began to give, and she closed her eyes while she tried to tap into her reserves of wilting composure.

She opened her eyes and gave a contemptuous smile. 'Almost as little as I'd want you as a friend.'

One corner of his mouth lifted in a sneer. 'Friendship is not possible between men and women.'

That he held this chauvinistic viewpoint did not surprise Sam at all. 'You *would* think that. It just so happens that one of my best friends is a male.'

'And sex has never got in the way…?'

He said it as calmly as if he was asking her how she liked her steak. Sam was less then comfortable about discussing sex in the same *county* as this man, let alone while he was touching her. She looked away, aware of the flush that had mounted her cheeks. 'I'm talking about Jonny.'

'So am I.'

Sam's horrified gaze flew to his face. 'All I am to Jonny is a s…supportive friend. I'm getting tired of telling you—there's never been anything like that between us!' she protested shrilly.

'And you wouldn't *want* there to be? Do not play the innocent with me. I have been watching you.'

'The all-knowing, all-seeing Alessandro Di Livio?' Sam cut in, her voice a successful marriage of boredom and amusement. Inside, however, she was struggling to control her rising panic. She lifted her chin, carefully focusing her gaze somewhere over his right shoulder to avoid contact with those hateful *knowing* eyes. 'In case you've forgotten,' she reminded him, 'Jonny is married.'

Alessandro arched an ironic brow and wondered if the copper hair felt as silky as it looked. 'I haven't forgotten.' His voice dropped to a low, threatening purr as he pushed his point home. 'And I suggest *you* don't.'

Sam felt the humiliating colour in her cheeks deepen.

Of course it wouldn't occur to him that she might have the odd principle or two. 'I've told you—Jonny and I are just good friends.'

A quiver of irritation crossed his olive-skinned face and he gritted something soft and angry in his native tongue.

'Well, let's just say your mouth says one thing…' He paused, a slightly distracted expression drifting across his face as his glance zeroed in on the soft full curves of her lips. 'And,' he continued, anger hardening his voice, 'those big, hungry eyes say another thing entirely. Have you been waiting for him to notice that you're a woman?' He released a low, scornful laugh as his eyes raked her stricken face. 'Of course it is entirely possible you wouldn't like it if he had,' he mused, half to himself.

'I wouldn't know—he never has!' Sam was pushed into yelling.

A moment later she connected with his eyes and wanted to curl up and die from sheer humiliation. But pride, and the scorn in his eyes, made her stick out her chin and pronounce in a low, but clear voice, 'But I'm not the type to give up at the first hurdle.'

His dark brows twitched into a disapproving straight line above his masterful nose. 'Are you totally without conscience?'

The irony made her laugh. *'Gosh!'* she sighed, holding up her hands in mock surrender. 'You've seen right through me. I'm your original scarlet woman. Your sons are not safe while I'm around.' Her lips twisted into a derisive grimace. 'For goodness' sake, you silly man, I don't represent a danger to anyone.'

He stiffened, and from where she stood she could distinctly hear the sound of his startled inhalation. Sam studied his face and thought, I'm guessing that nobody has ever called him a *silly man* before. More's the pity. If they had he might have learnt not to take himself so desperately seriously.

His dark eyes narrowed to slits, but the startled annoyance glittering in the dark depths was mingled with reluctant admiration as he registered the mockery shining in her eyes. 'You are a very aggravating female.'

She glared back up at him, torn between exhilaration and exasperation and wishing that he'd yelled—not used that purring tone which made more places than the soles of her feet tingle. 'And you,' she declared, dumping diplomacy in favour of bluntness, 'are much more likely to be the cause of the break-up of your sister's marriage than I am!'

His lips curled. *'Me…?'* He dismissed her words with a

shrug of his magnificent shoulders. 'You think you can shift the blame that easily?' A suspicious expression slid into his deep-set eyes. 'You are talking as though a break-up is inevitable…?'

When Sam turned her head away, her lips tight, Alessandro placed a finger under her chin and drew her face round to him. His narrowed eyes scanned her angry face.

'What do you know…?' he demanded, his voice dropping in volume in direct proportion to the degree of threat in his tone.

'Like I'd tell *you* if I did know anything,' she retorted, pulling her chin free.

Her breath coming in short, angry gasps that made her chest rise and fall in tune with her rapid respirations, Sam planted her hands on her hips and angled an angry glare up at him, her eyes flashing green fire.

'Oh, you *will* tell me…'

At that moment Sam was willing to do just about anything to wipe that confident smirk off his impossibly good-looking face. 'Brought your thumbscrews with you, did you?'

Before he could confirm or deny this a giggling couple carrying glasses of wine came around the corner. They saw Alessandro and Sam and stopped dead.

'Oops—pretend we're not here!' said the girl, grabbing her partner's hand and winking at Sam before she dragged him away.

'Oh, God!' groaned Sam, burying her face in her hands. 'Just what I need.' Pam Sullivan was the sort of gossip who could make the most innocent incident sound salacious.

'You're right—we need some privacy.'

Sam's head came up, her expression horrorstruck. She needed privacy with Alessandro Di Livio the same way she needed cellulite!

'That place over there—what is it?' He nodded towards a section of tiled roof just visible beyond a large shrubbery.

'It's the gazebo, I think.' The original intention had been for a band to be situated there, so that the guests could listen while they sat or strolled around the lovely grounds. Then the weather had intervened and things had been hastily transferred indoors.

'It will suit our purposes,' he announced.

God, if Pam had heard that it would have made her year. 'Look,' Sam said, deciding it was time to inject a little reality into the conversation, 'the only place I'm going is back indoors. I'm freezing cold, and this conversation—such as it is—is over.'

She froze and looked at the hand on her arm. A strong, shapely hand, with long, tapering fingers. Having it touching her without any sort of warning switched her brain into mush mode.

'Yes, you are cold,' he agreed, sliding one brown finger under the neck of her blouse. It slid slowly across the bony prominence of her collarbone before moving back to the hollow at the base of her throat. The blue-veined pulse there was throbbing so hard that he couldn't fail to feel it.

Had her brain not already been mush, she might have noticed that his fingers lingered there a lot longer than was strictly necessary—not that it mattered. The damage was done in the first micro-second of contact.

It had an electric effect—almost literally! It was, Sam mused, as she tried to focus her hazy thoughts, like being plugged into the mains. It took the space of a heartbeat for the shock to travel all the way to her curling toes.

'I don't want your jacket.' Actually, there were other things she wanted less—things like the surge of lustful longing that was making her ache in every cell of her body. But a lifetime of focusing on good things enabled her to look on the bright side: now that he was no longer touching her, her paralysed vocal cords had started working.

Acting as if she hadn't spoken—*no change there*—he carried on shrugging off the beautifully tailored pale grey jacket he wore. Draping it over her shoulders, he placed a hand in the small of her back and propelled her in the direction of the gazebo.

'You don't take no for an answer, do you?' His jacket retained the warmth of his body and held the faint, elusive fragrance that was exclusively him—a mingling of the masculine fragrance he favoured, soap, and warm male.

Standing there in his silk shirt, he appeared not to notice the cold—even though the fabric was fine enough for her almost to see through. She could definitely see the strategic drift of dark body hair on his chest, and the suggestion of muscle definition on his taut washboard belly.

Ashamed of what amounted to a fascination with his body, Sam—painfully aware that her cheeks were burning—turned her head to one side. Well, as far as she was concerned he could freeze to death—and good riddance!

'This is ridiculous,' she muttered under her breath, thinking, *He's not a man, he's a darned force of nature.* Despite the fact that saying no to him had as much impact as saying no to a hurricane, she was uneasily aware that she ought to have at least tried. The casual observer might have been forgiven for jumping to the conclusion that she actually wanted to prolong their time together.

A comment Emma had made not long after she'd met the man she was eventually to marry popped into Sam's head. 'You know, Sam, I have more fun fighting with Paul than having sex with any other man. Makes me wonder what the sex will be like… Actually, I started wondering *that* about five seconds after I met him.'

When Sam had admitted with a touch of envy that she'd never met a stranger who had that effect on her, Emma had laughed and said with total conviction that she would one day.

Though exposed on one side, the gazebo did offer some protection from the elements. Once inside, Alessandro took her by the shoulders and spun her to face him. Leaving his hands where they were, he looked down into her face.

CHAPTER FOUR

OH, GOD, did today have to be the day? And did he have to be this stranger?

'Why are you looking at me like that?' he asked.

I was trying to imagine what it would be like having sex with you, was clearly out, and she wasn't sure if her voice even worked, so Sam shook her head, and inside his jacket carried on trembling. She had no intention of surrendering to her darkest urges even had the opportunity arisen. And she supposed to some people the gazebo, tucked away from prying eyes, might represent that opportunity.

Actually, the fact she *had* dark urges at all was a bit of shock-horror revelation. The urges she felt for Jonny could not be described as dark, she mused. Those feelings were a lot more wholesome and easier to handle. Also, there was a certain safety in fantasising about a man who had never noticed you had breasts.

While Alessandro didn't like her, and actually seemed pretty much to despise her, Sam *did* get the impression he knew…

'This situation is easily resolved. Just tell me what you know.'

Shamefully aware of the ache and burning tingle in her shamelessly engorged breasts, Sam crossed her hands across her chest in a protective gesture. 'This is getting beyond ridiculous.'

'What is ridiculous is you thinking I'm going to let you go before you tell what you know about the problems in my sister's marriage. And don't tell me you don't know anything, because you look as guilty as hell.'

'And you look—!' She watched as his lashes dipped, casting a shadow across the slashing curve of his strong cheekbones, and the breath suddenly snagged in her throat. *You look perfect, damn you!*

She stepped back, and his hands fell from her shoulders. Still feeling the imprint of his light touch on her skin, she squinted angrily up at him. 'This isn't guilt,' she said pointing at her face. 'This is fear for my safety. You are obviously a total lunatic.'

'Then I suggest you humour me.'

Sam swung away, her hands gripping the lapels of his jacket. Her low heels clicked on the wooden floor as she walked to the opposite side of the octagonal enclosure to put as much space as was humanly possible between them. A faintly pointless exercise, as the sound of footsteps behind her indicated the wretched man had followed her.

'Fine!' she cried, throwing her hands up and turning to face him. 'The problem with Kat's marriage? Yes, there's a problem.' She jabbed a finger in the direction of his chest. 'Like I said—you.'

Alessandro looked at the small finger and felt a sudden distracting desire to lift it to his lips. 'I warn you, I *will* have an answer.'

'And I'm giving you one. Has Kat *asked* you to intervene in her marriage?'

In the act of dragging a hand through his dark and tousled hair, Alessandro stopped and slung her an exasperated look. 'What sort of question is that?'

Sam ignored the interjection. 'Well, has she?'

'Of course she hasn't.'

'And would she feel able to come to you if she needed to?' He looked indignant. 'Of course she would.'

'Then don't you think it might be a good idea to wait until

then before you jump in with your…' she glanced at his feet and added, '…size twelves? Kat is twenty-one,' she reminded him.

'She was *nineteen* when she got married. At nineteen she should have been—'

Sam actually felt a twinge of sympathy as he clamped his lips together and inhaled deeply through flared nostrils.

'You thought she was too young to get married?'

'Do you think at nineteen you should be deciding to commit yourself to one person?' he demanded scathingly. 'What were *you* doing at nineteen?'

She responded unthinkingly to the curious question. 'I was training to be a teacher.'

'And would your parents have been happy if you'd turned up at home married to some beach bum?'

'Jonny was *not* a beach bum—he was a champion surfer.'

'I stand corrected,' he inserted drily. 'Married to an ex-champion surfer.'

'My parents would have flipped,' she admitted. 'But it happened, so you just have to live with it. You know, *I* think Kat is pretty resourceful—and *quite* capable of sorting out her own life. It might be easier for her to do that if you weren't always there, hovering in the background like a bad smell.' Actually, he smelt pretty wonderful—but she felt the occasion called for a little poetic licence. 'Don't you think,' she asked him gently, 'that it's time you let go? Doesn't Kat deserve the chance to make her own mistakes?'

An expression of blank astonishment spread across Alessandro's face. 'You think *you* are qualified to offer *me* advice?'

'Not qualified, maybe,' she conceded, flushing at his sneering tone. 'But you asked. I know you have a close relationship with your sister—'

'You know nothing about it.'

'I used to wish I wasn't an only child, but meeting you has made me realise what a lucky escape I've had. Let me spell it out. The fact is you are no longer the person she's meant to turn to for support. Couldn't you settle for being emergency back-up rather than the main man? Have you any idea,' she wondered out loud, 'how intimidating you must be to a younger man?'

'*Intimidating…?*' he echoed, looking bewildered by her contention.

'What man could compete with the marvellous Alessandro Di Livio?' she asked, rolling her eyes.

His mobile lips thinned with displeasure. 'Don't be ridiculous.' Looking thoughtful despite his terse tone, he added, 'It isn't a competition.'

'Not to you maybe…' she inserted drily.

'I have never interfered in my sister's marriage.'

Sam stared at him, wondering how on earth he could say that with a straight face. 'Oh, pardon me. I must have imagined the past…' she glanced at her watch, her eyes widening '…half an hour.'

'It has felt like longer,' he gritted.

Under the capacious folds of his jacket, Sam folded her arms across her chest. 'You're being nasty because you know I'm right. You really shouldn't grind your teeth like that.'

She stood and listened in silent admiration as he loosed a flood of very angry-sounding Italian. If tone was anything to go by he seemed to have an extensive knowledge of expletives in his native tongue.

'If you're in love with Trelevan surely it would be in your best interests to see his marriage fail?'

The angry colour in Sam's cheeks deepened. 'Caring for someone obviously doesn't mean the same thing to you as it does to me. When you care for someone you want them to be happy.'

'*Care…?*' His lips twisted derisively as he spat the word. 'I am not talking about caring. I am talking about passion…lust…'

And I so wish you wouldn't! 'I think you're talking about sleazy sex.'

'And you? What are *you* talking about? Holding hands?' he suggested, reaching out and capturing one of hers. 'Picking out matching china and deciding on the new garden furniture?'

Angrily Sam tore her hand from his, praying that his no doubt well-developed predatory instincts had not told him what the contact had done to her. 'You're obsessed with sex!' *And it's catching.*

The claim made him laugh. 'Well, at least I don't have a problem with it.'

The taunt made her cheeks burn. 'I don't have a problem with sex—just you!'

'It makes you blush just to say the word…' he discovered, sounding astonished. 'I don't believe you have ever wanted someone so much that you would do anything to have them.' He angled a speculative look at her flushed face. 'When was it you decided he was the love of your life?'

'I'm not going to discuss Jonny with you.'

He gave a grimace of distaste. 'Give me honest lust rather than mawkish sentimentality any day.' His expressive upper lip curled. *'Look at me—I've got a broken heart, but what a little trouper I am…'* He gave a snort of disgust and shook his head. 'Heaven preserve me from women who fancy themselves as martyrs.'

Scenting a certain inconsistency in his criticism, she held up her hands. 'Hang on—I thought I was some sort of calculating, husband-stealing—'

'Frankly,' he said, dragging his hand through his dark hair in an exasperated manner, 'I'm not quite sure *what* you are.'

The way he was looking at her made Sam's throat grow dry. She pressed a hand to her throat, where her heart was trying to climb out of her chest.

'You have been generous with your advice…so let me give you some in exchange.'

She folded her arms across her chest and looked bored. 'This should be good…'

'Stop weaving your sexual fantasies around somebody else's husband and go out and get yourself a lover.'

This recommendation drew an inarticulate gurgle from Sam's throat. 'Jonny does *not* feature in my sexual fantasies!'

His eyes stayed hard and hostile while he bared his teeth in a wolfish leer. 'Then he definitely isn't the man for you.'

'I do not have sexual fantasies!' she choked.

'Then you really are as repressed as you look.'

Sam regarded him with loathing and prayed that one day he would tell a woman he loved her and she would laugh in his face. That such a woman existed was somewhat doubtful, but if there was any justice at all one day he would crash and burn—and she would be there to see it!

'Then you don't have to worry, do you? I'm too repressed to seduce your sister's husband. And, just for the record, I do not fancy myself a martyr,' she added, in a voice that shook with the strength of her outraged feelings. 'And I doubt if *you're* capable of anything deeper than lust—with anyone other than yourself, that is.'

The only response she got to her biting condemnation was a quirk of one dark brow. 'Are you surprised he has never noticed you are a woman when you dress like—? On every occasion I have seen you, you dress to hide your femininity, not celebrate it.'

'You mean flaunt?' Sam suggested, and gave a scornful laugh. Actually, she didn't find being thought dowdy and unattractive by a man who had to be about the most attractive creature on the planet nearly so amusing as she made out. 'I don't enjoy being leered at.'

One ebony brow lifted as he affected amazement. 'I'm amazed you have any experience of leering.'

Ashamed of the weakness which brought the hot sting of tears to her eyes, Sam gritted her teeth and glared up at him. 'Not all men are as shallow as you!'

'I think you'll find they are, *cara*.'

'Well, I wouldn't want the sort of man I have to tart myself up for and pretend to be something I'm not.'

'I think the idea is that the man should make you feel sexy and attractive. Hasn't any man done that for you?'

Sam pressed her hands to her ears and shook her head in a childish gesture of denial. 'If you don't shut up, I'll…I'll…!'

Her frustrated threat ignited a look of astonishment in his heavy-lidded eyes, and then, as he appeared ready to reward her audacity with a killer retort, he saw the telltale glitter in her eyes. 'You're crying…?'

Sam bit her lip and shook her head. 'You'd like that, wouldn't you?' she accused.

Without warning he reached across and took the hand she held clenched against her chest, raising it towards his mouth. 'I have no desire to see you weep. But that red-headed temper…it will get you into trouble if you don't learn to tame it.'

Fighting clear of the paralysis which held her a pliant spectator, Sam snatched her hand from his grasp and backed away. Her eyes trained unblinkingly on his face, she carried on backing up until the backs of her legs made contact with a wooden chair. She let out a small shriek and stumbled, and would have fallen if a strong arm hadn't snaked around her waist.

'You should be more careful,' he cautioned.

A shaky laugh squeezed its way past the emotional congestion in her aching throat. 'That sounds like excellent advice,' she said, fixing her eyes on a point mid-way up his chest.

His dark, autocratic features were hard and remote as he posed his question. 'You love him…?'

Very aware of the arm still encircling her waist, she cleared her throat. 'I'm not about to discuss my feelings with you.' *So what have you been doing for the past half an hour?*

'What I don't understand is why you stood back and let her take him?'

Sam felt something inside her snap. Her head came up. *Let*

her…? He made it sound as though she'd had some sort of option.

'What would you have had me do?' she demanded, stabbing a finger within a whisper of his broad chest.

'Do…?' he said, watching the accusing finger with an expression of fascination.

'Well, you seem to be the expert.' She angled her head, directing her resentful glare into his lean face and stepping backwards. The fact that she wanted to protest when his hand fell away only made her angrier.

'How would *you* go about making someone notice you?' She recognised the total stupidity of her question the moment the words had left her lips.

As if anyone was not going to notice him!

Let's face it, the man was a total hunk—with more rampant maleness in his little finger than most men had in their entire bodies. He was the perfect male specimen—from the top of his sleek, glossy head to his highly polished shoes. Her resentful glare slid from his bronzed, beautifully sculpted features and skidded over his lean, lithe frame. Some men might wear a suit to disguise a few unwanted inches around the middle, but not him. Even sheathed in perfect tailoring there was no disguising that Alessandro's body was in perfect condition.

'I thought such things came naturally to a woman,' he offered suggestively.

Sam sucked in a furious breath through her clenched teeth. 'There's nothing *natural*,' she sneered, 'about push-up bras.' Glaring at him, she clamped her hands over her not terribly impressive breasts. 'Or, for that matter, comfortable—and besides, this has nothing whatever to do with underwear.'

'You were the one who introduced the subject,' he pointed out mildly.

'What would *you* have suggested? That I flaunt a bit of leg?' she asked, extending one slender appendage in his direction. A snort of disgust escaped her lips as she shook her hair back from her hot face. 'Take up pole-dancing?' she challenged.

His dark eyes travelled up the slender curve of her calf. 'An interesting thought,' he murmured, swallowing. 'But it probably wouldn't have done you any good if there was no chemistry to begin with.'

'For your information, I wouldn't *demean* myself just to get a man,' she declared hotly. Then aware that his eyes were fixed on her hands and what they covered, she dropped them and added, 'I suppose that's the sort of thing you like? Women who make fools of themselves to get your attention?'

His dark brows lifted to a quizzical angle. 'You consider it demeaning to seduce a man?'

'*Seduce…?*' she echoed, as an image of herself astride the prone figure of a man, running her fingers down his lean, hard torso flashed through her mind. The image itself was deeply disconcerting. The fact that the man in question was Alessandro was utterly shocking.

'It is what a women who is worthy of the name would do to get the man she loves,' he contended calmly. 'It is certainly a more healthy option than clinging to a juvenile infatuation.'

'I'm not infatuated with anyone,' she choked, thinking that if she could curse anyone with unrequited love it would be this man.

Continuing to scan her upturned features, his only response to her protest was a smile that made her want to hit him.

'You spend too many evenings alone with your romantic dreams. Sex isn't about soft focus and sweet music,' he derided scornfully. 'Sex is visceral. It's about smells and texture…' Without warning he reached out and ran a long brown finger down the inner aspect of her wrist. Sam gasped as the light contact sent an electric shock through her body.

When she finally got her paralysed vocal cords to respond, her voice seemed to be coming from a long way away. 'Thank you for the lesson…' She had no doubt at all that he was a master of the subject.

His mesmerising eyes locked onto hers and Sam felt her knees shake.

'It's about sweat.' His low, throaty purr had an almost narcotic quality, and Sam, aware of the danger it presented, was seduced by it anyway.

She might not like the man, she might loathe what he was and what he stood for, but she wasn't crazy enough to imagine she had been granted some sort of immunity to the raw sexuality he exuded.

Painfully conscious of her wildly quivering stomach muscles, and aware that she was quite literally panting—which could give the wrong impression—Sam fought to control her breathing, perfectly aware that there was nothing mutual about the chemical reaction she was suffering. How could there be? Compared to the sexy, in-control women he dated, she must seem like a sexless reject…an oddity.

Sam sniffed and lifted her chin to an aggressive angle. At that moment if she had been granted any wish she would have blown it without a second thought for that special X factor that made some women totally irresistible to the opposite sex—or at least *one* of the opposite sex.

Well, let's face it, Sam, the only place you're going to be able to say no when he begs you to be with him is in your dreams.

'If I want sweat I'll go to a gym,' she retorted, just managing to sound derisive even though her knees were shaking.

The longer this confrontation went on the stronger the feeling became that she was a voyeur rather than a participant in the scene. She shivered and released a scared gasp as his half-closed eyes moved over her slender body.

'What you need is some reality,' he concluded.

His thickened accent nailed her to the spot. Was there anything short of a Lotto win that was *less* real than discussing sweaty sex with Alessandro Di Livio? *'Reality…?'* A shaky laugh emerged from her lips, sounding reckless when in reality she had never felt less reckless in her life.

'What I don't need,' she panted hoarsely, 'is advice from *you!*'

'What you need is some…' his heavy-lidded eyes touched her mouth and his own lips quirked '…*substance.*'

'Next you'll be telling me that what I need is you…' Her scornful laugh faded as he took her face between his big hands, and she thought, *Did I invite this…?*

As he looked at her wide, soft pink mouth, a sound that was close to a growl vibrated in his throat. Sam felt the vibration and opened her own mouth to say something frosty and ascerbically cutting, which would awaken him to the fact that he wasn't dealing with one of his simpering push-overs, but encountered his glittering eyes. All her life her cutting one-liners had saved her from uncomfortable situations, yet now, of all times, her ability to deliver a slick comeback had failed her!

The last time she had seen that much barely restrained heat had been in a disaster movie about a volcano. She became aware of the fact that she was no longer cold—no longer cold to the point where she was burning up.

'If you kiss me I'll sleep with Jonny,' she hissed.

CHAPTER FIVE

OF COURSE she realised too late that this wasn't the sort of man who responded well to threats—even empty ones. Only he didn't know it was empty, because he clearly considered her a trollop when he wasn't thinking she was frigid. His entire attitude towards her was decidedly schizophrenic.

Alessandro cupped the back of her head in one hand and drew her face up to his. This was one of those moments that definitely required a verbal bucket of cold water to stop a bad situation getting worse.

A moment where Sam knew she had to send him a very strong, unambiguous message.

Moaning and grabbing his jacket while she gasped, 'Oh, God!' was not the message she had intended to send! But it was either that or fall down at his feet, so she chose the option which was on balance marginally less humiliating.

His long fingers moved through the strands of hair, grazing her scalp and causing several million nerve-endings to sigh as she inhaled the warm male scent of his hard, lean body. There was an expression of fierce fascination in his face as he let the silky strands fall through his fingers, making Sam's senses spin.

'Your hair should be hot,' he rasped throatily.

Why not? The rest of me is. She was burning up from the inside out. Common sense told her that there were no flames burning in his utterly spectacular eyes, but knowing it was a mirage didn't stop her stomach dropping to somewhere below her knees.

'I really think… Oh, God…' She sucked in her breath sharply as he moved his thumb across her trembling lips. 'The thing is, you don't have to do this…'

It didn't take a genius to work out his sudden interest. He thought if he kissed her she would forget about Jonny and start lusting after *him*. An inconvenience he was no doubt prepared to put up with for his sister's sake!

Her heavy lids lifted when he stopped what he was doing—something which Sam was dismayed to discover she had mixed feelings about. Blinking, her passion-glazed eyes wide and wary, she glimpsed for a split second his expression. She thought he looked shocked, then a short, strange laugh was wrenched from his throat and he bent his head towards her.

'The thing is, though, I find I do.' His expression suggested that the discovery didn't make him overwhelmingly happy.

'But I'm not going to seduce Jonny,' she protested weakly. 'And if I did,' she confessed, 'he probably wouldn't notice. He doesn't think of me as a girl…'

Alessandro focused on the curve of her lower lip, which was hard to do without biting into the luscious pink softness. 'Not even *he* is that much of an idiot…' he said, thinking he probably was.

'He is… That is, no, Jonny's not an idiot!' Sam protested. 'You just don't understand—'

Alessandro's angry voice cut across her faltering defence of the man she was clearly infatuated with. 'I don't want to understand,' he informed her tautly.

'But you…' The raw, driven intensity of the way he was looking at her made the words dry as her aching throat closed over.

'The only thing I want to do is taste you,' he confided, in

a rough velvet drawl that made every individual cell of her body ache with a deeply disturbing nameless need. 'And I'd prefer you didn't talk about another man while I do it.'

'Don't I have any say in the matter?'

She stopped, her expression freezing as she realised that she wanted to kiss him. She wanted him so much that she could feel it in her bones. And, actually, what harm could it do?

My God, am I even considering letting this man kiss me? Could I stop him? And, more to the point, do I want to stop him?

Well, it might be interesting. Actually being kissed by a man who was hard and lean, who smelt delicious and male and… Sucking in a horrified breath, she brought her private debate to an abrupt halt. *Interesting…!* God, I'm going insane—stark, staring mad!

Alessandro gave a fierce smile and ran a brown finger along the moist inner curve of her lower lip. 'I don't generally ask permission before I kiss a woman,' he confessed, before reaching up and calmly unfastening the clip that held her hair in a careless topknot on her head.

Too astounded by his action to do anything, including breathe, she stood there, her shocked gaze trained on his face, while her hair tumbled around her shoulders. He reached out and lifted a hank of shiny coppery hair, winding the tendril around his finger before he released it. 'You should always wear your hair loose. Why would I ask for permission to kiss you when it is obvious that you want me to?'

'You're insane!' And he's not the only one, she thought as she grabbed her hair in both hands before pushing it ruthlessly behind her ears. 'If you go around doing this sort of thing I'm amazed you've not been arrested yet.'

He looked amused by the accusation. 'It's the signals you're sending out. Though you're probably not even aware of doing so,' he conceded. 'Your pupils are dilated and your skin is flushed.'

'So is yours.' There was a faint sheen to his glorious olive-toned skin, and bands of colour accentuated the sculpted elegance of his prominent cheekbones.

'You look like you'll taste…sweet,' he observed, his breathing quickening perceptibly as he stared at her lips in a way that made Sam's sensitive stomach flip and quiver.

'That would be the strawberry cheescake…' she responded, faint, but holding it together in a pulse-racing, knee-shaking sort of way—until she made the mistake of allowing her darting gaze to linger on the sensually moulded curve of his mouth. 'Cheesecake,' she echoed, getting hot inside as she carried on staring at his mouth and thought about how it would feel on her skin. 'Do I have some on my mouth…?' She touched the tip of her tongue to her lips, very aware of and mortified by the heat spreading through her body.

Alessandro sucked in his breath through flared nostrils, and the reckless, predatory gleam in his hooded dark eyes made Sam's already stressed pulse kick up another notch. She brought her eyelashes down in a protective shield and plucked fretfully at the neck of her shirt, to loosen the fabric that was clinging to her damp, hot skin.

'The only thing you need on your mouth is mine…' he claimed, with the sort of macho arrogance that should in theory have brought a scornful laugh to her lips.

But this wasn't theory, and it was no theoretical tongue that slowly traced the outline of her quivering lips and tilted her face up to his. Paralysed with lust, she literally ached for the taste of him. The man didn't have many things right, but in this particular instance, as she felt the first movement of his lips against her own, Sam could find no fault with his conclusion. She *did* need his mouth on hers.

Oh, God, did she need it!

Her lashes lifted from her flushed cheeks when his head lifted. *'Oh, God!'* she moaned, meeting his hot, glittering eyes. 'I suppose you think that proves something? Other than the fact you can kiss quite well.' Which had always been pretty much a given. Nobody with a mouth like his could be a bad kisser.

One corner of his fascinating mouth lifted. 'Let's see if I can improve on *quite well…*' he rasped, placing one hand on the back of her head and the other on her bottom. He put his lips to hers and jerked her towards him in one smooth motion.

Sam felt something inside her explode as the erotic pressure increased until she could bear it no more, and with a groan she opened her mouth and moaned into his mouth. As they kissed with a wild, frenzied hunger that Sam had never experienced or dreamt existed she pressed her body into his, drawing herself up onto her toes to slide her fingers into his hair.

When his head lifted it was small comfort that he looked almost as dazed as she felt. She stared at him, her eyes big and shocked, and rubbed the back of her hand across her swollen lips. On legs that felt like cotton wool she took a shaky step backwards.

'Why did you do that…?'

Good question. 'If you kiss Trelevan—no,' he corrected. 'If you go near him, I will wring his pathetic neck,' Alessandro promised grimly, knowing that she cared for the other man's safety and comfort a lot more than she did her own.

Well, now she knew why he had done it. Her own motivation was much less clear-cut. 'You are a manipulative bastard.' *And I am a total push-over.* 'And if you lay one finger on me ever again—'

'You'll say, *Don't stop,*' he inserted smoothly.

A wave of mortified colour washed over her milk-pale skin as she stared up at him with loathing. 'I'll sell my story to the tabloids.' As empty threats went, this one was pathetic. He obviously thought so, because she could hear the sound of his laughter as she walked away.

Sam kept her back rigid and her head disdainfully high until she shut herself in a booth in the powder room. She was in there half an hour all told, what with crying and then fixing the damage to her face.

When she emerged she had concluded that it would be a mistake to get hung up over a kiss… It was nothing major—just a wrinkle.

She almost believed it.

CHAPTER SIX

'LISTEN, Em, I should be making a move.'

'Now! But it's still early,' Emma protested, raising her voice above the gentle buzz of conversation and the music supplied by a string quartet from the local music college. 'What have you done to your hair?' she added, looking at the skewed knot on the top of her friend's head.

Sam, whose efforts to repair the damage had been severely hampered by shaking hands and a need to mouth *You idiot* at her reflection in the powder room mirror every two seconds, ignored the question.

'I want to get back before it gets dark.' Sam felt guilty when her friend's face dropped, but stuck to her guns. She was pretty sure that if called upon to make polite small talk with Alessandro she might make a total fool of herself. Whether this would involve slapping him or begging him to kiss her was a matter she didn't want to think too hard about!

'I thought you were staying with your mum and dad tonight?'

That was before one of your guests kissed me and I kissed him back. 'Change of plan.' She flashed a smile. Her guilt injected a couple of extra million volts into it.

Emma took in the brilliance and grinned back. 'What's his name? Do I know him? Are we talking husband material?'

An image of Alessandro's dark, devastating features flashed into Sam's head. Anything *less* like husband material would be hard to find. Some women would just look, but there would always be those ready and willing to lead him astray.

She wasn't saying being totally gorgeous to look at automatically made a man incapable of fidelity, but it would take a woman who was supremely confident in herself to be able to take the covetous stares of other women in her stride.

The woman who married Alessandro would have to be a supremely confident creature or totally gorgeous—probably both. In short the female equivalent of him.

'I had a phone call…publisher…' She shrugged.

Emma looked dissatisfied by her response, but beyond subjecting her friend to an uncomfortably searching look made no further protests beyond, 'Well, you definitely can't go without saying goodbye to Paul. When last seen,' she revealed with a smile, 'he had retreated with half the other men to the Orangerie. I think they're talking cricket.' She rolled her eyes.

'Lead on,' Sam said, picking up her handbag and following her friend down the plush carpeted corridor that led to the Orangerie. Emma's husband, Paul, and half a dozen of the other male guests were indeed there, but they weren't talking cricket. They were huddled in one corner displaying varying degrees of horror and discomfort as they watched the object responsible for the ear-splitting din that Sam had heard halfway down the corridor.

When Sam had last seen the blond-haired three-year-old he had been enchanting the adults with his sunny smile and a lisping rendition of a nursery rhyme. Now he was lying in the middle of the floor, his red tear-stained face contorted with fury, as he screeched and drummed his heels on the floor.

On seeing his wife, Paul Metcalf hurried across. 'Thank God you're here, Emma. It's Harry. Simon got a call, and he asked me to keep an eye on Harry for a minute.'

'How long,' Emma asked, wincing as the toddler hit a high note, 'has he been like that?'

'It feels like hours,' her harassed husband responded dourly.

Emma exchanged glances with Sam. 'I think he needs his mum. Do you know where Rachel is, Sam?'

Sam shook her head. 'Shall I go and look for her?'

Despite the fact that Rachel, whose father was the local vicar, was a couple of years older than both herself and Emma, the three girls had always been inseparable. And, unlike many childhood alliances, theirs had not fizzled out when they reached adulthood and went their separate ways. Rachel, who combined a career in banking with being wife to a very dishy New Yorker, had asked Sam to be godmother to Harry, her firstborn. When she had uprooted and followed her husband to the States the previous year both Sam and Emma had visited, but had been delighted when Simon's firm had decided to resettle them in London.

Paul caught Sam's arm. 'No, you stay here. I'll go,' he offered eagerly, before his wife told him very firmly to stay put.

Sam paused before going to console her godson, her amused glance sliding around the group of men. 'Didn't it occur to any of you lot to *do* anything for the poor little mite?'

'Have you seen the state of him?' her indignant host demanded, speaking on behalf of the other men present. 'There is enough chocolate cake on that kid to feed the five thousand, and I'm wearing my best suit. And,' he added, eyeing the flailing legs, 'the "poor little mite" has a kick like a mule.'

'*Wimp!*' his wife retorted scornfully.

'This situation obviously calls for the female touch,' Paul observed with dignity. 'Either that or a good child psychologist,' he added under his breath.

Emma caught his arm. 'You think so?' she said. 'Look at that,' she invited, venting a loud, incredulous laugh as she nodded towards the prone toddler. '*He* doesn't seem too bothered about getting *his* suit dirty. My God—this is marvellous!'

Along with Paul, Sam turned in time to see a tall, elegant figure squat down beside the screaming youngster. She watched in total amazement as Alessandro, balancing on his heels and appearing totally unfazed by the pandemonium or the risk to his designer suit, began to talk casually to the screaming toddler.

'The man has guts—I'll give him that.' Paul's brows knitted as an expression of horror spread across his face. 'Our sweet little Laurie is never going to do anything like that, is she…?'

Ignoring her husband's worried enquiry, her fascinated gaze trained on the man and baby, Emma said knowledgeably to Sam, 'It's a cultural thing. Mediterranean men have no problem showing affection to babies and children—unlike our homegrown variety…' she added, directing a scornful sniff towards her spouse.

Alessandro carried on talking as he loosened the knot on his tie. Sam was too far away to make out what he was saying, but the child obviously could, and it appeared to have an immediate and nothing short of magical effect on the distraught youngster.

'My God!' Emma breathed, as the child's cries became noticeably less strident, then faded totally. 'What is he saying, do you suppose?' she wondered in an awed undertone.

The child lifted his tear-stained face towards Alessandro and chuckled.

Sam didn't respond. For some insane reason, when she saw Alessandro respond to the child with a smile that made him look relaxed and at least ten years younger, she got an empty, aching feeling in the pit of her stomach.

'Come!'

Responding to Alessandro's imperious command and to his open arms, the toddler climbed into them without a moment's hesitation and wound his grubby hands around the man's neck.

There were several gruff murmurs of appreciation as Alessandro got to his feet.

The genuine quality of Alessandro's smile became—to Sam's mind, at least—forced when he noticed her. Sam, the lapel of her criminally unattractive suit clasped in one hand, expelled a gusty breath and tried to act as if every nerve in her body wasn't screaming.

Beautiful man…baby…the whole thing was so painfully clichéd she would have to be a total idiot to fall for it. But falling she was… Oh, what is *wrong* with me? I must be one of those women who are only attracted when there's no chance of their feelings being returned, she decided. Even if in this case they were shallow and lustful. A shrink would have a field-day dissecting my twisted psyche.

'That,' declared Emma, walking up to Alessandro and ruffling the toddler's blond hair, 'was very impressive. I'm glad I invited you now.'

Alessandro's dark eyes creased at the corners as his smile warmed the dark depths. Sam, whose nerve-endings were twanging like an overstrung guitar, knew that if he ever smiled at her that way she was in deep trouble. *And you're not now?*

'You weren't glad before?'

'You were welcome as Kat's big brother before, and now you're welcome because you are a brave and resourceful man who laughs in the face of danger.'

'It's always nice to feel welcome,' Alessandro responded, his dark, heavy-lidded eyes briefly flickering in Sam's direction.

Sam, her heart thudding wildly in her chest, pretended not to notice.

'Shall I take Harry?'

Emma didn't argue when he shook his head and said, 'Harry would like to find his mum, and if the route should take us anywhere near ice cream this would not be a bad thing.'

Sam looked at the smear of chocolate down his cheek, at the sleek hair ruffled by childish fingers, and her indignation escalated. Alessandro looked so damned relaxed and at ease with a grubby, cranky kid on his hip…How *dared* he slip out of the hedonistic playboy role she had assigned him?

'No idea where Rachel is,' Emma admitted. 'But as for the ice cream, I'll get that for you myself…'

At that moment Rachel, wrapped in her habitual air of unruffled serenity, walked into the room. She took in the situation at one glance.

'I take it from the glazed looks that you have been treated to one of Harry's grade A tantrums? Goodness, Harry,' she reproached, as her son wrapped his arms limpet-like around her neck, 'you'll put Aunty Sam totally off having children,' she observed, flashing Alessandro a warm smile as the transfer of grubby child was smoothly completed. She arched an enquiring brow as she lifted her eyes to the tall Italian. 'It looks like I have you to thank Mr Di Livio…'

Alessandro gave a self-deprecating shrug. 'Not at all. Harry and I were just becoming acquainted and discovering a mutual fondness for ice cream. Now, if you'll excuse me… Oh, and ladies…' the voltage of his smile switched up several notches as he added firmly '…it's Alessandro.'

'If you don't have children,' Emma called after him, 'it will be a total…no, a *criminal* waste!'

Without breaking stride Alessandro flung her an attractive grin over his shoulder. 'I am not married.'

'Where were you three years ago?'

'Being cited in a divorce case,' Sam muttered. Did Marisa Sinclair, who had lost both her husband and her lover, regret her affair? Sam wondered. Or did she consider it a price worth paying?

'Sam, how could you? I'm sure he heard you,' Emma remonstrated as the tall, dark-headed Italian vanished from view.

Sam gave a defensive shrug. 'What if he did? And what do you mean, *how could I*? *You* don't like him.'

Rachel stood looking bewildered by this uncharacteristic display of childish venom. 'Did I miss something?'

'Sam doesn't like the gorgeous Alessandro,' Emma explained. Rachel laughed as she expertly wiped excess chocolate from around her son's mouth. 'That much I *had* gathered. Well,' she conceded, 'he's not the sort of man who inspires *liking*, is he?' She gave a naughty grin and added, 'Personally, I think he's rather sweet.'

'Sweet?' Sam echoed, staring at her friends as though they'd lost their minds. 'He's not sweet,' she hissed. 'He's a snake!'

Emma and Rachel looked at their normally good-natured friend in amazement. 'What has the poor guy done to you?' Emma asked.

Goaded, Sam yelled, 'The *poor guy* kissed me!'

Sam registered the identical looks of shock closely followed by delight that spread across her friends' faces, and with a groan closed her eyes. 'Pretend I didn't say that,' she begged, knowing there was little to no chance of her plea being heeded.

'You and Alessandro...' Emma drew a shuddering breath. *'Wow!'* she gasped enviously. 'I'm assuming that he is a *very* good kisser. How could a man who looks like *that* not be...?' she concluded logically.

'He,' snipped Sam crossly, 'would be the *first* person to agree with you.'

Emma looked totally unperturbed by the loathing in Sam's retort. 'I sort of thought he would be...I bet he's something in bed.'

'Don't look at me!' cried a pink-cheeked Sam, flinging up her hands in exasperation as she gazed balefully at her best friends. 'I've no intention of finding out.'

Rachel grinned. 'Well, I call that mean. You're a free agent, and what have Emma and I got left except enjoying a sex life vicariously through our friends? And, let's face it, Sam, so far your love life has not exactly been any compensation.'

'So sorry,' Sam drawled. 'Look, you two,' she added uneasily, 'you're not going to make a big thing out of this, are you? It was nothing...absolutely nothing.'

'Nothing that's got you pretty hot under the collar… Oh, all right,' Rachel placated as Sam gave a frustrated groan. 'We'll be the souls of discretion,' she promised, miming a zipping motion across her lips, as she winked at Emma.

By the time Sam had extracted the spare tyre from her boot she had been supplied with ample evidence that the age of chivalry was dead and buried. The only attention her plight had gained so far had been honks on the horn from several lorries. She had been trying to figure out which way up the jack went for five minutes when a car actually pulled up. Her knowledge and interest in cars was, to put it mildly, limited. The one that had drawn up was big and black and to her uneducated eye looked expensive.

Brushing her drenched hair from her eyes, she peered through a sheet of rain which was falling horizontally… If it wasn't a man behind the wheel it was a very large female.

Just my luck!

A woman would have been much less likely to dish out patronising stuff about clueless female drivers in this situation, and with a woman she wouldn't have had to worry about the sleaze factor. Oh, well, she thought, giving a stoical shrug. This was a situation that called for a lot of smiling and teeth-gritting, and if necessary the defending of her virtue…that was if she wanted to get back to town before she drowned—and she did.

And when you thought about it, it was her own fault. If she didn't want to be treated like a stereotypical helpless female she should have picked the car maintenance evening class and given Italian Summer Cooking a miss.

Knowing your way around a risotto is *not* going to get you home, Sam…so smile nicely and book in to the next car maintenance class.

'Hello, there—' Sam broke off, her jaw dropping as she identified her rescuer. 'You!' she ejaculated in disgust.

It was definite. Fate was having a laugh at her expense!

'This is your spare wheel…?' Alessandro pulled up the collar of his jacket and with his toe nudged the tyre, where it lay on the ground.

'Go away!' Sam snarled from between gritted teeth.

The broad shoulders lifted in one of his inimical shrugs. 'As you wish.'

Sam watched as he turned and began to walk back to his car. Almost bursting with indignation, she ran after him. 'You're just going to leave me like this?' she yelled.

He stopped and turned. 'Was that not what you wanted?'

Her eyes narrowed. 'You're such a creep!' she declared forcefully, then added, 'And don't think I'm not perfectly capable of putting on my own tyre.'

'Not *that* tyre.'

'Yes, that tyre.'

He shook his head and looked so smug that she wanted to scream. 'That tyre has no tread.'

She looked at him blankly.

'It is illegal.'

A flicker of uncertainty crossed her face. 'It looks fine to me,' she muttered mutinously.

'It is useless—actually, worse than useless. Because in this weather the only place it will get you for sure is the nearest casualty department.'

'You're exaggerating,' she charged.

He gave another of his magnificently expressive shrugs. 'It's your neck.' Halfway through turning, he swung back. His eyes slid down the pale column of her throat before he added harshly, 'I suggest, if you feel unable to accept my help, that you ring the nearest garage.'

Sam bit her lip. She knew the admission was going to make her look even more of an idiot than she already did as she fished her phone from her pocket and grunted, 'My battery is low.'

He released a long hiss of irritation and wrenched open the door of his own car. 'Get in—I will give you a lift.'

Sam, who had been looking wistfully at the luxuriously upholstered interior, stiffened at the terse invitation. There was a militant glitter in her aquamarine eyes as she released a scornful laugh. 'You think I'd get into a car with *you*…?'

'Don't you think it is a little late to display caution?' His nostrils flared as his eyes swept across her upturned features. 'I find it staggering,' he revealed, in a voice that suggested he was trying *very* hard not to yell, 'that an apparently *intelligent* female should act with such wanton disregard for her personal safety.'

'What do you mean?' No man had a right to look that good with his hair plastered to his skull…but she was forgetting it wasn't just *any* skull—it was the *perfect* variety. God, she thought, it would be so much easier not to loathe the wretched man if you could discover one minor imperfection.

'*Dio…!*' he gritted. Muttering under his breath in angry Italian, he let his head fall back, revealing the strong lines of his supple brown throat. Then, as she stared through the rain and the mesh of her spiky lashes, he dug both hands into his drenched sable hair and pulled it back in a way that sent water streaming down his olive-skinned face and neck.

Sam, unable to tear her eyes from the spectacle—which oughtn't to have been erotic but was—felt things move deep inside her. Unspecified, but deeply disturbing things. She reluctantly recognised that something far more worrying than the rain was responsible for the drowning, breathless sensation she was experiencing as she watched the water glide over his smooth brown skin.

Alessandro's head came up, and guiltily her eyes dropped. Jaw clenched, he glared at her downbent head. 'You have been standing at the side of a lonely road, fluttering your eyelashes…'

The injustice of this harsh accusation brought her head up. The first thing her distracted gaze lighted on was the silvered drops of rain trembling on the tips of his own preposterously long eyelashes.

Eyelash-fluttering would get *him* further than it would me, she thought.

'I haven't…' Her voice faded away as her eyes connected with his.

'And,' he continued, once she had lapsed into silence, 'inviting the attention of any psychopathic lunatic who happens to drive by. You either have an unhealthy addiction to danger or you have no sense of self-preservation whatever. I suspect both,' he concluded grimly.

The awful part was, he had a point. 'Well, I'd prefer to get into a car with a psychopath than you!' she blurted out childishly. Then, lowering her eyes, she added in a small voice, 'Could I use your phone?'

At that moment another articulated truck went by and blasted its horn.

Alessandro followed the vehicle with his eyes until it vanished from view over the brow of the hill. When he turned his attention back to her his jaw was set and his eyes held a steely look of determination.

'Get in!'

His attitude did not suggest compromise, but she'd try anyway. She looked at his mouth, and her defences slipped just enough to let through one forbidden thought. *I kissed that.*

If she got into that car who was to say she wouldn't repeat the performance? *Chance would be a fine thing.* She took a deep breath and told herself sternly that thinking that way was going to get her into trouble.

'If you would just let me use your ph—'

'Get in, or I will *put* you in,' he interrupted, not sounding like a man with kissing on his mind. 'I have no intention of being interviewed by the police as the last person who saw you alive.'

Sam paled a little at the image his brutal words conjured. 'There's no need to be so dramatic.'

Ignoring her scornful complaint, he swivelled his eyes significantly towards the door of the car. 'I do not have all day.'

Sam hesitated. 'You wouldn't…?' Their eyes met and she gulped. He would.

I need therapy, she decided, appalled by the gut-tightening excitement in her belly. When did I turn into the sort of woman who gets turned on at the idea of being man-handled? Her eyes ran up the long, lean length of the man who stood there radiating impatience, and she thought, Not *any* man.

With as much dignity as a person who was literally dripping could muster, she arranged herself in the front seat as he stood and watched. His expression suggested that the outcome had never been in question.

Did people always do what he wanted? she wondered as she snuggled down into the cream leather upholstery. She looked blankly at the hand he'd inserted.

'Keys…I need to lock up your car. Not that it would be the car of choice for most self-respecting car thieves,' he said, sliding a contemptuous look towards her ancient Morris Traveller.

'It's a classic,' she said, dropping the keys into his palm. 'And it has character.'

'It's a heap. And it doesn't go,' he contradicted, before slamming the door.

Cocooned from the rain and wind, the quiet interior of the car felt like the eye of a storm. Despite the relative warmth, she shivered as she became conscious of the clammy coldness of layers of drenched clothes against her skin.

She tried to wring some of the excess moisture from her hair while she examined her surroundings. Nice—but then you'd expect Alessandro to travel first class—and big too, she thought, stretching her legs out. Big, but not nearly big enough. Her heart started to beat out an erratic tattoo against her breastbone as she thought about spending any time in such close proximity with him.

It stood to reason there must have been an alternative solution to her dilemma, that didn't involve being touched by Alessandro or locking herself into a confined space with him. Quashing the growing sense of panic she felt as she looked around the interior of the car, she closed her eyes and reflected on the unfortunate fact that around him she acted like someone suffering from oxygen deprivation.

She was wondering whether it might not be better to brave the elements and any passing bad guys when the door was wrenched open. She stiffened as the interior of the car was for a moment filled with cold wet air, followed by the elusive male scent of the exclusive fragrance he favoured.

'Here,' he said, handing her the keys.

'Thanks,' she said, fumbling as she tried not to touch his fingers. She lifted her head in time to see him shrug off his drenched jacket.

A sigh shuddered through her body. *Oh, my God!*

His white shirt had been rendered totally transparent by the rain, and clung like a second skin, revealing every individual muscle and hard contour of his lean, bronzed torso. Her breathing quickened as she tore her fascinated gaze away from the tantalising shadows created by drifts of dark body hair.

'Take your coat off,' he suggested, casually slinging his own jacket into the back seat.

She shook her head and clutched at the lapels of her knee-length pink trench coat. 'No, thanks,' she croaked. 'You could drop me at the first service station. There's one in the next village along, I think.'

He slung her an impatient look before pulling off the grass verge. 'Two petrol pumps and a tin hut, as I recall. Even if they *did* happen to be open for business at nearly eight p.m. I doubt if they'd retrieve your car until the morning.'

'Eight…?' Her expression shocked, she glanced at the watch on her wrist. She hadn't realised until that point how long she had been standing there. Lips pursed, she slid him a belligerent look. 'I suppose you think I should say thank you?'

'Not if it's too painful.'

'The tyre *was* bald…?' She looked at his hands on the steering wheel, then looked quickly away as she felt the muscles in her abdomen tighten. Her sensitised nostrils quivered. The car was heating, intensifying the disturbing scent of warm, wet male mingled with the subtle fragrance Alessandro favoured. Short of not breathing, it was impossibile not to inhale the heady concoction.

'Totally.'

Looking out of the window, her posture rigid, Sam missed the amused sideways glance he slid her.

'Why would I lie about such a thing?' he asked. 'Unless, of course, you think this is all part of a plot to have you at my mercy?'

'Very funny.'

'You are cold?'

Sam, who was very conscious of the trickles of sweat running down her back, shook her head.

'Then why are you shaking?'

'I'm not,' she lied. Then, because she clearly was, she added gruffly, 'My clothes are wet.'

'How long were you standing in the rain?'

'I'll be fine. I'll have a nice bath when I get home.' Anticipating the luxuriant soak that lay ahead, she sighed— and missed the flare of heat in his eyes as they swerved briefly from the road ahead.

The silence between them, which wasn't anything close to cosy or comfortable, stayed unbroken until he drove straight past the turn-off for the motorway a couple of miles farther down the road.

'This isn't the right road.'

'It is for where we are going,' he responded, with aggravating calm.

Sam glared at him, bristling with suspicion. Just as she was about to demand an explanation he slowed, and with a display of fast reflexes avoided a cat that darted across the road. The action made her think of the accident which had killed his parents. Had it been difficult for him to get in the driver's seat again? If it had you certainly couldn't tell from his calm, competent manner at the wheel of the big powerful car.

'I saw that programme last night,' she confessed, without thinking.

He slanted her a quick sideways look.

'About the accident…' she added, when he didn't respond.

'It was exploitative rubbish.'

For once she was in total agreement with him. 'Yes, I know.' She looked at his flawless profile and added, 'I'm glad you don't have any scars…physical ones, that is. Not that I'm implying that you have mental scars, but anyone would… Oh, God, if I was writing this I'd delete those last few lines of dialogue.'

To her amazement he laughed, and said, 'I do.'

'You do what?'

'I do have physical scars. You just haven't seen them…*yet.*'

Threat or promise—whichever it was, the result was the same. Desire clutched low on her belly as she struggled to lock the whimper that fought to escape in her throat.

Do not go there! Sam told herself. The sexual tension crackling in the air was too strong to ignore, but maybe if she didn't react to it, it might go away…? She turned and stared out of the window, and wondered how much more of this her nervous system could take before she burst into flames!

A few moments later the probability of spontaneous combustion became all the more probable when he observed casually, 'We need to get a room.'

CHAPTER SEVEN

Now, this she couldn't let ride.

'You need your head examined,' she rebutted huskily. 'If you assumed that just because I kissed you—' she gave a mocking laugh and was grateful he had no idea of the images playing in her head '—I'm going to *sleep* with you!'

'I suggest you wait until you're asked before you say no.'

The humiliating colour flew to Sam's cheeks as she turned her head back to the window, cursing her unruly tongue.

'I'm not saying it won't happen—'

'I really couldn't be that lucky…' she drawled sarcastically.

Alessandro grinned, but didn't turn his head. 'I like to prioritise.'

'You sweet, spontaneous romantic, you.'

Again he grinned. 'I had no idea you wanted me to be romantic. I assumed you just wanted me for my body. Seriously.' He slanted a quick sideways glance at her huddled figure. 'You urgently need to get into some dry clothes. There's a place a mile or so down here where I sometimes stay. You can take a hot bath while they dry your things.'

Sam released an incredulous laugh. This high-handed behaviour was clearly par for the course for him. 'It didn't occur to you to ask me if I *want* to go there?'

He looked mildly surprised by the question. 'Not really.'

'Do people always do what you tell them?' she wondered out loud.

'You would prefer to be wet and uncomfortable?'

Sam, very aware that her saturated clothes were chafing in several places, gritted her teeth. 'That's not the point…'

'On the contrary—it is very much the point. I realise that you would prefer to walk barefoot over hot coals than fall in with any suggestion *I* make…'

'It wasn't a suggestion, it was a *fait accompli!*' she snapped.

He angled a dark brow. 'You noticed?' He congratulated her. '*Fait accompli* rather makes this conversation pointless, wouldn't you say? Why don't you give in gracefully? We can even pretend that it was your idea, if you like.'

Glaring at his smug, patrician profile, Sam lapsed into seething silence as he turned through a pair of big wrought-iron gates. The hotel's impressive driveway was a mile long, and led through some charming parkland where deer grazed in the fading light.

When Alessandro opened the passenger door Sam, who was staring at the big sprawling half-timbered building they had pulled up in front of, shook her head. 'You can't walk into somewhere like this and demand a room for an hour. They'll think…'

Alessandro gave a sardonic smile. 'They'll think what…?' The malicious amusement glittering in his dark eyes made it impossible for her to maintain eye contact. 'That we could not contain our mutual lust until we got back to London?'

'Don't be disgusting!' she choked.

'This display of puritanical outrage might carry more weight with me if you hadn't tried to rip off my clothes once already today. Perhaps it is *me* who should be concerned about *my* reputation?' he suggested, the gleam in his eyes becoming more pronounced as a fresh wave of mortified colour rushed to her cheeks.

'Reputation!' Sam yelled, leaping soggily from the car. Feet crunching on the gravel, she advanced, her small fists clenched. 'I think *your* reputation is beyond further blackening,' she sneered. 'What has it taken…? Ten years…? Still, I'm sure the effort was worthwhile. I think everyone knows by now that you're a sleazy, womanising loser! And as for ripping off c…clothes…' A distracted expression slid into her eyes as the memory of her hands sliding under his shirt and over hard, satiny-smooth skin flashed into her head. It was the wrong time to recall how warm and solid and male… She inhaled and shook her head, reminding him angrily, '*I'm* the one missing two buttons.'

It wasn't until she saw the direction of his gaze that Sam realised that in pulling open her jacket to reveal the gaping section of her shirt she had also unintentionally revealed a section of smooth, pale midriff. With an indignant squeak she dragged the fabric of her jacket together.

His smouldering eyes locked onto hers, and the simmering silence that stretched between them tore her already traumatised nerves to shreds.

'Relax—they don't rent rooms by the hour here. And besides, I keep a suite,' he revealed casually.

Relax? After what he had just said! Sam almost laughed. 'You keep a suite…?' she echoed incredulously. 'You live in a hotel?'

'Not live, obviously, but it is useful.'

Sam, who didn't see how a hotel off the beaten track in rural Cornwall could possibly be useful to a man who spent his time flitting from one European capital to another, looked sceptical. 'How often do you actually use it?'

'It varies. Twice…maybe three times…' He began to look impatient with her interrogation.

'A month…?' It seemed shockingly extravagant and wasteful to Sam. But then she wasn't a millionaire—or was that a billionaire…?

'A year,' he corrected, and her jaw dropped.

'*A year!*' She shook her head, unable to disguise her disapproval. 'That must cost a fortune.'

'You are lecturing me on fiscal imprudence…?' His expression suggested the idea amused him.

'It's nothing to me how you choose to spend your money. You can burn it for all I care.'

'If it makes you feel any better, I am joint owner of the hotel…a silent partner.'

Sam looked at his hand, extended in a silent invitation for her to climb the shallow flight of steps that led to the porticoed entrance where a tall figure had emerged from the building. The woman, her grey hair tied back in a smooth knot at the nape of her neck, was wearing a silk shirt and tweed skirt.

'What are you doing standing there?' She peered over the top of her half-moon spectacles, subjecting Alessandro to a critical glare. 'This poor child looks perished.'

To Sam's astonishment, far from going into one of his haughty freeze-you-with-a-glance routines, Alessandro smiled—the sort of heart-flipping smile that he probably reserved for the select few he genuinely gave a damn about.

The possibility that her own heart was utterly susceptible to the warmth of that smile brought a ferocious scowl to Sam's face.

She felt a hand in her back, propelling her up the steps, and heard him say, 'Sorry, Smithie.'

Smithie?

Inside the wood-panelled hallway, which didn't boast the usual reception desk, it was blissfully warm. The moment she stepped in, even before she had had an opportunity to register that the décor was 'lived-in country house', Sam was conscious of the warm, comfortable laid-back atmosphere. Despite the fact that her stress levels were off the scale, she felt some of the tension slip from her shoulders.

While Alessandro warmly embraced the older woman Sam

examined her surroundings curiously, conscious as she did so of the loud ticking of a grandfather clock set against the wall and of the distant murmur of conversation interspersed by the occasional laugh somewhere close.

'You look marvellous, Smithie. Like a fine wine, you improve with age.'

'One of the advantages of being an ugly young woman is that your face becomes more acceptably interesting as you get older.' Pushing Alessandro away with a sharp admonition not to drip on the carpet, she turned her attention to Sam. 'And who is this you have brought to see me?'

Sam, still bemused at seeing Alessandro spoken to as though he were a grubby schoolboy, blinked as the interrogative blue eyes swept over her. The woman personified her mental image of a girls' school headmistress—the sort that probably didn't exist outside a film-maker's imagination. She had the smallest and sharpest eyes she had ever seen. But I bet you don't miss much, Sam thought as she endured the searching scrutiny.

As Alessandro placed a hand lightly on her shoulder and drew her forward Sam caught sight of the crackling flames of an open fire through the open double doors to the right. 'This is Miss Samantha Maguire.'

Very conscious of the fingers on her shoulder, Sam nodded and flashing Alessandro a sideways glance, corrected him. 'Sam.'

'Well, hello, Sam Maguire. I'm Dorothy Smith—I manage the place.'

'Smithie is the non-sleeping half of the partnership,' Alessandro explained.

Considering the amount of energy the older woman exuded, Sam wouldn't have been surprised to learn she didn't sleep at all!

'My mother's family have lived in this house for centuries. When she died—' She broke off and sighed, adding, 'If it hadn't been for Alessandro's intervention it would have had to be sold to pay the death duties.'

'I know a sound investment when I see one.'

The older woman lifted her brows and laughed before turning to Sam. 'He had to sink a small fortune into it just to stop it from falling down,' she confided, slanting him a challenging look that dared him to contradict her. 'On present performance it will be another ten years before our hard-headed business tycoon even breaks even. Sound investment! Huh!' She snorted.

'I'm in for the long haul,' Alessandro said, looking as close to uncomfortable as Sam had ever seen him.

'Of course you are, dear,' the older woman agreed. 'Now, introductions over. What you need is a hot bath and a brandy, Sam,' Dorothy announced briskly. 'No, Alessandro,' she said, accompanying her sharp words with a dismissive wave of her hand as he began to follow them, 'we don't need you.'

Now, *that* was something he couldn't hear very often, thought Sam, torn between outright shock and amusement as she turned her head to see how he was taking the rejection.

Alessandro inclined his dark head, accepting the prohibition with an uncharacteristic meekness that made Sam's jaw drop. He intercepted her astonished stare and an ironic glitter entered his eyes.

'Come along, Sam…'

It amused Sam that the older woman's words were an order, thinly disguised as a request.

'I will see you later,' Alessandro said as she approached the broad sweep of the stairs.

'Now, there's something to look forward to.'

Her muttered response drew a quizzical look from the older woman, but she made no comment beyond recommending Sam to watch her step. Deciding to take this ambiguous comment literally, Sam lowered her eyes and clasped the curved banister.

She was eaten up with curiosity as to how this most un-likely of partnerships had come into being, but couldn't work out a way of asking without coming across as nosy. 'Are you very busy at the moment?' she asked, as a couple emerged from a room along the hallway.

Her hostess gave a nod, before asking Sam. 'Have you known Alessandro long?'

Obviously the other woman did not share her concern about appearing nosy. 'Not really. Actually, I don't really know him at all. I've been aware of him, of course…' She stopped, a dark blush spreading over her fair skin. 'Not aware in *that* way—just…' Lowering her eyes from the other woman's amused, knowing glance, she bit her lip. 'My car broke down—hence the drowned rat look.' She laughed. 'And he picked me up.' That, she decided, could have been phrased better.

'Oh, yes—he would,' the other woman said immediately. 'Alessandro is very chivalrous.'

Are we talking about the same man? Sam wondered, re-sponding to this affectionate confidence with a non-commit-tal grunt.

'I have known him since he was a child. I was his nanny.'

'Oh, that explains it!' Sam exclaimed without thinking.

'His mother was still travelling a lot with her work then…' The sharp little blackcurrant eyes scanned Sam's face. 'You did know that she was an opera singer…?'

Sam shook her head. 'No, I didn't know that.' It occurred to her that she didn't know much at all about Alessandro. But then, she asked herself, why should I? Bottom line was, he was the next best thing to a total stranger.

'Oh, yes, she had a very successful career. But after little Katerina was born she decided to become a full-time mother, and I was not needed.'

'That must have been hard for you.' Sam, who imagined that a nanny would become very attached to her charges, sympathised.

'Yes,' admitted Dorothy Smith. 'It was.'

'And for the child too…?'

The observation brought a flicker of approval to the older woman's eyes. 'It was,' she admitted. 'But he always kept in touch. Alessandro was always a punctiliously polite boy, and he wrote me delightful letters. I have kept them all. One day,' she promised, sending Sam a warm glance, 'I will let you read them.'

Embarrassed that the other woman persisted in misinterpreting her relationship with Alessandro, Sam bit her lip. Before she had a chance to set matters straight once and for all, the other woman continued.

'When the accident happened I had retired.' She shook her head, her expression sombre as she thought about those dark days. 'Of course I came back to help—though the first task was convincing Alessandro he needed help.' She stopped outside a door and smiled warmly at Sam. 'But I'm sure I don't need to tell *you* that.'

Sam just smiled. She suspected anything she said was not going to alter the other woman's determination to see a relationship where there was none. Hopefully, Alessandro would put her right. What was she thinking? *Of course* he'd put her right. It would do his reputation no good at all for people to think he was sleeping with a ginger-headed frump who wore beige.

'Alessandro usually uses that one, but the bedrooms are identical and of course they are adjoining,' Dorothy was saying when Sam tuned back into the conversation.

'Bedrooms…?'

'Yes, they're adjoining—see,' she said, pushing open a door. She saw Sam's expression and frowned. 'You could have a room of your own, of course, but with the Food Festival and the fishing tournament falling in the same week this year we're totally full.'

'Goodness, no—I just meant to say, I'm not staying. I'm going back to London tonight.'

'Really?' Her barely discernible brows rose. 'I must have misunderstood. I thought Alessandro said he was staying over.'

'Maybe he is—he's a free agent—but I'm not… Staying, that is—not not a free agent. Which I am—' She broke off, lifted a hand to her head and sighed.

The other woman observed her pale, drawn face and looked remorseful. 'Look at me, chattering on when what you need is some peace and quiet. I'll send you up some brandy. Now, off you go and get out of those wet things. The bathrooms here are really marvelous—when I think what the plumbing was like when I was a girl…' Shaking her head she lifted a hand in farewell and left Sam alone…finally.

Lying in the deep bath, her senses soothed by the decadent oils she had added to the water, Sam's thoughts turned to the day's extraordinary events. Her mind, pleasantly blurry from the shot of brandy she ought to have refused—though it would have taken a very strong person to say no to the redoubtable Dorothy—kept returning again and again to that bone-melting kiss.

She had not known that kisses like that one existed! Let alone realised what she had been missing!

Now she knew, and it had been Alessandro who had been the catalyst—the man who had been in the right place at the right time and pressed all the right buttons.

'It could have been anyone.' The room was empty, so the only voice of dissent to this defiant statement was in her own head. *Are you sure about that…?*

She sat upright, her expression mutinous and set. 'Too right I'm sure. There's nothing special about Alessandro Di Livio.'

The sheer ludicrousness of this contention drew a pained laugh from her throat as she slid back into the water. Alessandro was a lot of things, but commonplace was *not* one of them…!

Approaching twenty-four and she had never lost control…now, that was worrying. Even more worrying was the fact that she had not seen the appeal of such a loss until now! A part of her wished that the searing kiss had never happened, that she was still walking around in blissful ignorance, but another part of her was inclined to relive the moment again and again…!

Recalling once more those initial moments of boneless, melting submission made her heart-rate quicken. As Alessandro had plundered her mouth the submission had given way to something equally outside her experience: a frantic, inarticulate need to touch and taste…to fuse with his male heat and hardness. Thinking about the primitive response made her breathing quicken and her pale, translucent skin turn a rosy pink.

Sighing she sank beneath the water. Surfacing moments later, she brushed the fronds of water-darkened hair from her face. She *knew* she loved Jonny. It had been a given in her life for so long that she just hadn't questioned it—not until Alessandro had put doubts in her head with his sneers.

'I *do* love Jonny!' she announced defiantly to the steamy bathroom.

Just because you couldn't imagine yourself having steamy head-banging sex with someone it didn't mean you didn't love them! And, by the same token, just because you could imagine it, it didn't mean you did!

No, the stuff with Alessandro was just about sex. Maybe, she thought, lifting her head as the depressing possibility struck her, you couldn't have love *and* sex. You had to settle for one or the other. Now, that was a depressing thought.

CHAPTER EIGHT

SHE was belting a big fluffy robe when there was a tap on the interconnecting door. Without waiting for her to respond, the door opened and Alessandro walked in.

'What—?' she said, her voice accusing, because his presence sent her hard-won composure straight out of the window.

'I did knock,' he observed, dropping the jacket he was carrying on the bed and walking towards her.

'The idea of knocking is that you wait for someone to invite you in…or tell you go away.'

'You don't want me to go away.'

His calm assurance made her want to hit him. Lips pursed, she lowered her eyes. He had changed into a pale cashmere sweater and dark, close-fitting jeans, he smelt of soap and himself, and he looked sexy enough to cause mass hysteria in the female population of a small planet!

'Believe that if it makes you feel happy.' Tightening the belt on her robe, she was reminded of the fact she didn't have a stitch on underneath.

'I didn't come here to fight with you,' he said, sounding weary. 'I came to ask what you want to do about dinner. Do you want to eat here, or with the other guests? Though I must warn you up-front that a quiet dinner downstairs isn't an option. Smithie favours dining dinner-party-style.'

'I don't want to eat full-stop. I'm going home.'

'Don't be stupid—you must be hungry.'

Sam's eyes narrowed. 'Don't call me stupid.' She glared into his eyes and lost the plot. He had such gorgeous eyes— dark and deep and so, *so*…sexy…they made you want… Gasping sharply, she pulled herself up before she lost it completely. 'So you know,' she said, 'what I'd really like…?'

'What?' he asked, thinking she looked so pale and brittle that she might break if handled roughly. But he knew she wasn't that fragile. She hadn't felt breakable when he had held her in his arms. She had been supple, strong, and so very, *very* hot.

'I'd like you to leave right now.' *Before I do something very stupid.* 'Walk out of that door and never come back.' Her problem was she was in danger of believing there was something between them. *The only thing between us is two years of not liking one another.*

While they had been talking he had been moving towards her and she had been retreating, matching him step for step. Of course his steps were bigger than hers, and by the time her shoulders made contact with the wall and she could retreat no farther he was so close she could see the fine lines radiating from the corners of his eyes.

'You don't mean that.'

'I do,' she said, putting as much conviction into the lie as she could.

Alessandro, the strong bones of his face drawn taut against his golden skin, regarded her pale face in silence before his eyes dropped. 'If you tell me you're not interested I'll walk away.' His eyes lifted, and she was pinned beneath a taut, combustible stare that made the muscles in her abdomen quiver.

Sam blinked to clear the rash of red dots that danced across her vision, conscious as she did so of the heavy thrum of blood as it beat through her body. Chirpy, she told herself. You need to aim for chirpy, but firm.

Fingers crossed, she scrunched up her face in a mask of determination as she told herself over and over… *You can do it; you can do it…!*

She opened her eyes, and he looked so damned gorgeous standing there, so dark and lean and excitingly dangerous, that her will-power almost crumbled. My God, but being virtuous and sensible was not all it was cracked up to be, she thought dully.

'I'm not…interested.' She failed miserably with chirpy, but by some freaky accident she hit bored and couldn't-give-a-damn dead centre!

Other than a slight clenching of his muscles no visible re-action to her reply registered on his strong-boned, autocratic features. When he responded a moment later his tone was coloured only with an easy come, easy go quality.

At least I know I definitely made the right call, she thought.

Just because she'd decided that it was time she moved on with her life and stopped being faithful to a relationship that had never existed outside her imagination, it didn't mean her personality and values had changed beyond recognition.

She was realistic. She hadn't been walking around with her eyes and ears closed. She knew that for a lot of men—and, for that matter, women—sex had the same emotional content as a trip to the gym or a game of squash! A lover, yes. She recognised that she did have needs that weren't being fulfilled. But casual sex—no.

Am I expecting too much? It's not as if I'm asking for a life-long commitment!

It wasn't too much to ask to expect the man you went to bed with to at least remember your name the next day. She didn't want him to sleep with her because it was a rainy af-ternoon and he had a couple of hours in his diary to kill. Or, even worse, because he wanted to make sure she wasn't climbing into his brother-in-law's bed!

Alessandro scanned her heart-shaped face for a moment, his expression inscrutable, then after a slight hesitation in-clined his dark head. 'As you wish.'

Sam nodded back and thought, *Wish…!* If this was about wishes I'd be underneath you now…or maybe on top…

'You've been very kind,' she heard herself say stupidly.

That she could say anything at all with the sort of erotic images that were jostling for position in her head was nothing short of a miracle.

He flashed her a hawkish glare that was not at all kind. As he proceeded to consult the metal-banded watch on his wrist Sam's attention was drawn to the contrast of the cold dull metal to his warm, bronzed, satiny skin. Her stomach did a painful flip as she looked at the light dusting of dark body hair on his sinewed forearm and, appalled by the strength and primitive quality of the urge that made her want to touch him, she turned her head.

You just have to step back, she told herself. *Be objective…!* Great advice—pity there's not a chance in hell of me taking it, she thought, swallowing the bubble of hysterical laughter in her throat.

Inhaling a deep, sustaining breath, she made herself focus on his face. The line between his strong dark brows deepened, as though his thoughts had already moved on to more pressing issues. Of course it was good that he'd accepted her decision and not tried to dissuade her, but she would have felt a little better if he had looked as though it cost him *some* effort!

Obviously not sleeping with me ranks alongside other minor inconveniences—such as missing the last post!

It was just beginning to dawn on her that he'd been standing there looking at his watch for a strangely long space of time when he lifted his head and looked at her.

'If you do want to go back to London tonight speak to Smithie. She will arrange transport.'

'You're not going back…?' His eyes narrowed fractionally and she added quickly, anxious to dispel any impression that she was trying to invite herself along for the ride, 'Not that I expect a lift or anything.'

His hand on the door, Alessandro turned slowly back. Sam gave a sharp intake of breath and shrank back from the molten ferocity of the expression that drew the flesh taut across the sharp angles of his lean face. *'A lift? Madre di Dio!'*

'No, it's fine. I'll probably give my mum a ring and stay at home until my car is sorted.'

His narrowed obsidian gaze moved across her face. 'You stand there looking like that and talk about getting your car fixed!' He closed his eyes, pressed his fingers to the bridge of his patrician nose and released a wrathful flood of fluid Italian.

Italian, Sam decided, listening in awestruck silence to the outpouring, was a very expressive language to get mad in. Though for the life of her she couldn't figure out what she had said or done to trigger this from a man who was legendary for his reserve and control. When he opened his eyes again she realised that she wasn't seeing the polite regret she had felt was being expressed moments earlier. In his searing stare she was seeing overt raw hunger and rampant frustration… Not an *I missed my game of squash* expression at all.

As Sam's stomach muscles clenched she suddenly wasn't so sure about her assessment of the situation. Alessandro wasn't acting like a man who was going to forget her name by tomorrow. He was acting like a man who was pretty near to losing it!

As she studied him through the spiky sweep of her dark lashes she saw him rake a hand viciously through his hair. As he padded across the room, as sleek and dangerous as any jungle cat, she could hear him muttering under his breath in his native tongue. Having put several feet between them, he turned his head and looked at her.

My God, but he really is magnificent! The tightness in her chest became a physical pain as she watched him.

'You think I could trust myself to be alone in a car with you?' The frustration emanating from him was an almost palpable entity in the room.

Sam, not knowing what else she could do or say, shook her head.

His sensual upper lip curled in a grimace of self-derision. '*Dio,*' he rasped thickly. 'I can't trust myself to be in the same *room* as you!'

It wasn't until after the door had slammed, hard enough to rattle the hinges and several pieces of artwork on the walls, that Sam, her emotion-whacked body limp, literally crumbled. Tears streaming down her face, she slowly slid down the wall until she sat in a hunched heap of misery on the floor. A sob of titanic proportions rocked her body as her head fell forward into her hands.

Why on earth did you tell him to go?

Sam had no idea how long she sat there. The next thing she registered was strong hands tilting her face upwards and dark eyes filled with concern examining her tear-drenched features.

Alessandro had dropped down onto his knees beside her.

'Tell me,' he demanded, his velvet voice roughly imperative. 'What is wrong?'

'Nothing…' she claimed, with tears still streaming down her face. 'What are you doing here?' *Other than driving me totally out of my mind.*

'Clearly *nothing* is a lie. I left my jacket.' His eyes didn't leave her face as he nodded towards the bed. 'Now, tell me,' he coaxed. 'No, I know,' he added harshly. 'And the man is not worth it. I know it seems hard now, but if you can forget…'

'*Forget?*' she shrilled, pulling her face angrily from the protective circle of his fingers with a loud sniff. 'How the hell am I meant to forget when *you're* here.'

He pressed a hand to his chest and looked confused. '*Me…?*'

'Who else?' she demanded, rubbing her teary eyes with her balled fists.

'You were crying before I returned.'

'Of course I was. You left!' Her lips started to quiver as a fat tear slid slowly down her cheek. *I never cry.*

Alessandro dragged a not quite steady hand through his hair and looked mystified. 'Because that is what you wanted.'

'My God, are you *stupid?*' she yelled, glaring up at him through a shimmer of tears. With both fists she scrubbed the dampness from her cheeks and then, as her eyes slid from his, admitted huskily, 'I lied.'

'You lied…?'

She nodded and sniffed. 'About not wanting you to stay.'

He tensed and leaned back on his heels, his eyes fixed on her downbent head.

'I didn't want you to go…' With a groan, Sam lifted her head, pushing her still damp copper hair back from her smooth forehead as she met his eyes. 'Well, I *did*—but I didn't…'

A muscle in his lean cheek clenched and then clenched again as he fought the impulse to crush her to him. *Per amor di Dio!* A man would have to be lacking every red blood cell not to respond to the sultry half-scared invitation in those wide-spaced eyes. Despite the fact that his body ached he held himself in check…*just.*

His seething frustration concealed behind a languid fa-çade, he smiled sardonically. 'Well, that makes everything as clear as mud.'

Female mood swings were something he had a healthy masculine respect for, but this woman was in a class of her own! He had always prided himself on his self-control, but if she changed her mind again he feared that his control—already tested to the limit—would prove inadequate to the task of walking away. The women he had mutually beneficial arrangements with knew the score; there were no emotional scenes. By contrast, the red-headed Samantha Maguire was a walking three-act drama!

His ironic drawl ignited a flare of anger in Sam. *What does he want me to do…? Beg…?*

Alessandro watched her white teeth sink into the trembling

curve of her full lower lip. He swallowed. *Dio mio,* it was more than flesh could bear! He had been thinking about that mouth all day, and what he would like to do with it.

Hands clenched at his sides, his thoughts abruptly reversed to the moment earlier that day, when he had witnessed Trevelan kissing her. His primitive desire to choke the life out of the younger man had, he reasoned, been a perfectly legitimate response when the honour of his sister was concerned.

The only problem with that was that Alessandro hadn't been thinking of Katerina—at least not at that moment. He had seen the other man kissing Sam and his first thought had been, *That should be me.* His thoughts were running along the same lines at that moment.

Lifting her chin to a belligerent angle, Sam choked bitterly. 'I thought you were supposed to have a brilliant brain? Do I have to spell it out?' She heaved an exasperated sigh.

He angled a dark brow as his smoky gaze moved across her face, lingering longest on her pink parted lips, before he produced one of his inimitable shrugs and said, 'Maybe…'

'Maybe you'd like me to put it in writing?' Then there would be permanent proof that she was such a push-over where he was concerned that she was totally shameless. That she was ready to beg and he hadn't even touched her. *If he did touch me…* Gulping, she tore her gaze from his long brown fingers. But it was too late. Every nerve-ending in her body was already screaming for attention.

'Then why did you tell me to go?'

For a bright man, she thought, he could be dense at times.

'Because you put me on the spot,' she told him accusingly. 'Because you made *me* the one to make the decision when all I wanted you to do was…'

'What did you want me to do?'

She shrugged and her eyes slid from his. 'Kiss me, I suppose.'

'If you wanted to be kissed, telling me you weren't interested probably wasn't the best clue.'

'Well, I didn't actually know how much I wanted you until you walked away.'

The dark colour scoring his chiselled cheekbones deepened as he inhaled sharply. 'And do you still want me?'

She swallowed and lifted her eyes. The smouldering heat in his made her dizzy, and totally, utterly reckless. 'Only slightly more than I want to breathe,' she confessed huskily.

Alessandro took her face between his hands, allowing his thumbs to move across the smooth contours of her cheeks. 'I think we can arrange for you to do both.'

Breathing hard, Sam turned her head and kissed the open palm of his hand. 'You do know that you've got everything a perfect lover should have…?'

Alessandro stopped what he was doing and studied her flushed face with a fascinated expression. 'Are you going to tell me what those qualities are?'

'You're beautiful—not that you being ugly would be a deal-breaker, exactly,' she conceded. 'Because you've got bucket loads of sex appeal. And you're not going to insult my intelligence by pretending to be in love with me or anything…'

'You don't want love?'

She was suggesting the sort of mutually beneficial relationship that he favoured—so why did he not feel pleasure, even relief…? Actually, he couldn't quite pin down the cause for his perverse gut response, and now was not the moment for deep soul-searching. Alessandro, in the grip of a blind, relentless hunger unlike anything he had felt since adolescence, had more urgent matters to consider—like the very real possibility he might go insane if he didn't bury himself deep inside her in the near future!

'I thought I did, but you've made me look hard at myself.'

He looked startled by the confidence and framed a cautious question. '*I have…?*'

'You know what I do on Saturday nights?' He shook his head, but Sam's head was too filled with images of her unsatisfactory life to notice the strangeness of his expression. 'What I want,' she told him, 'is to be more like you. I have needs,' she told him, 'and I want to have sex without feeling guilty.'

'With anyone in particular?'

She stuck out her chin and thought, If he laughs, I'll die. 'You, for starters.'

He didn't laugh, or even contest the 'for starters'. Instead he grabbed her by the shoulders and yanked her towards him. Then, teasing her lips with his mouth and tongue, he took her face between his hands. His mouth came down hard on hers and Sam melted bonelessly in his arms.

CHAPTER NINE

As HE sat on the edge of the bed, slipping off his shoes, Sam reached out and touched his dark hair. The thick, lustrous texture fascinated her. Raising herself up onto her knees, she pulled his head round towards her and pressed her lips to his in a long, lingering kiss.

'You taste incredible,' she sighed against his mouth, and ran her finger down the stubble that darkened his strong jaw. 'Rough…'

'I need to shave twice a day.'

The smoky glow in her eyes deepened as she caught her tongue between her teeth and sucked in a long sultry sigh. 'Not on my account. I like it.'

'Madre di Dio!' groaned Alessandro, breathing hard as the dark lashes lifted from her flushed cheeks to reveal her passion-glazed eyes. 'Hold that thought,' he instructed imperatively.

Sam smiled and plastered her shaking body to his back. The heat and hardness of him through the robe was shocking, and more exciting than she could have imagined was possible. She felt his lean body tense and he inhaled sharply.

'You are impatient.'

Who wouldn't be? She'd been waiting twenty-four years for this moment. She just hadn't realised it until now.

Sam let out a tiny startled shriek as his hands closed around her wrists, and a breathless moment later she found herself sitting, or rather lying, across his lap. His head bent towards her and she closed her eyes and moaned low in her throat as she opened her mouth to the skilful incursions of his tongue.

'God!' she groaned, suffocating with desire as he kissed his way down the curve of her neck. 'I must have been mad to say no to this.'

Alessandro stopped what he was doing long enough to look at her with hot, hungry eyes and insert huskily, 'I didn't go very far.'

'And you came back,' she whispered, sliding her hands under the thin cashmere sweater he was wearing. A jerky little sigh was snatched from her throat as she made contact with the smooth, warm, hard flesh of his belly. 'You're so…' She sighed as, eyes half closed, breath coming in short shallow gasps interspersed by little moans, she let her hands glide palms flat over his satiny skin.

Sam felt the contraction of his stomach muscles as he sucked in a sharp breath, his hands tightening over her bottom as he gave a deep moan of pleasure.

'I'm awfully glad you came back.' His skin felt like oiled silk, and it was deliciously warm.

There was a long dragging silence before he confided, 'So am I.' Taking both her wrists in his, he drew them from his body and brought them to his mouth.

'I want…'

He stilled her protest by the simple expedient of kissing her, a deep, drugging kiss that left her weak and wanting more…*much more.*

'You shall have what you want. You shall have everything you want,' he promised huskily.

As their gazes locked, the dark promise in his heated stare made Sam's heart thud even harder against her ribcage. Alessandro released her wrists and then, still holding her gaze, lifted his jumper over his head in one smooth motion

GET FREE BOOKS and a FREE MYSTERY GIFT WHEN YOU PLAY THE...

SLOT MACHINE GAME!

Just scratch off the silver box with a coin. Then check below to see the gifts you get!

YES! I have scratched off the silver box. Please send me the four FREE books and mystery gift for which I qualify. I understand I am under no obligation to purchase any books, as explained on the back of this card. I am over 18 years of age.

P6EI

Mrs/Miss/Ms/Mr	Initials	

BLOCK CAPITALS PLEASE

Surname _____

Address _____

_____

Postcode _____

7 7 7	**Worth FOUR FREE BOOKS plus a BONUS Mystery Gift!**
🍒🍒🍒	**Worth FOUR FREE BOOKS!**
♣♣♣	**Worth ONE FREE BOOK!**
🔔🔔🍒	**TRY AGAIN!**

Visit us online at www.millsandboon.co.uk

The Reader Service™ — Here's how it works:

NO STAMP NEEDED!

THE READER SERVICE™
FREE BOOK OFFER
FREEPOST CN81
CROYDON
CR9 3WZ

NO STAMP
NECESSARY
IF POSTED IN
THE U.K. OR N.I.

and flung it across the room, revealing the sleek, hard contours of his bronzed upper body.

Sam's rapt gaze dropped, desire clutching like a tight fist low in her belly, and she thought, *You're the most beautiful thing ever—flawless.* The academic interest she had decided she was going to adopt towards her first real sexual experience became a dim and distant memory as she started to shake from head to toe, and she didn't even realise she had voiced her thought until he said, 'Thank you, but I am not without flaws.'

Not understanding the odd inflection in his voice, Sam felt a frown form between her brows. She reached for him, but to her frustration he levered himself off the bed in a fluid motion. Taking two steps away, he turned back to face her.

'What's wrong…?' The tension that had begun to build between her shoulderblades seeped away as he began to unbuckle the belt on the jeans that clung to his long, muscular thighs, only to be replaced by another sort of tension.

Touching her tongue to the beads of sweat that had broken out across the curve of her upper lip, she felt the feelings that he had aroused in her coalesce into a sexual desire so raw and primitive it pushed every other consideration from her head.

As he kicked aside his trousers he held her eyes.

The lustful surge that slammed through her body was so all-consuming that it was a few moments before Sam registered the scars that ran the length of his thigh. Unable to stop herself, she gasped. 'From the accident?'

Sam had watched the programme, had seen him looking barely alive on the stretcher, but until that point she hadn't considered his injuries. Those scars spoke of many weeks and months of pain and suffering. They spoke of a long and difficult period of rehabilitation.

Her throat closed over as she thought of him going through that alone. Her hands tightened into fists. *Dear God, let there have been someone there for him.*

His flat voice was totally devoid of emotion as he asked, 'You find the scars repulsive…?'

The dry question brought a rush of furious colour to her cheeks. 'Do I look shallow and stupid?' she demanded.

He studied her face for a moment in silence, and then, although his expression didn't alter, she sensed he relaxed. 'You look…' His eyes darkened as they slid slowly over her recumbent form. 'You look incredibly desirable and sexy.'

'*Oh…!* So do you, actually.'

His eyes glittered. 'How well suited we are.'

That, she thought, sucking in a breath as he lowered his long, lean frame beside her on the bed, remains to be seen. *It could be that I'm going to be really awful at this.* Was it really wise to begin with someone who must have pretty high standards? Of their own volition her eyes dropped to the bulging evidence of his arousal, barely contained by the boxers he wore.

'Still my fiercest critic…?'

Sam's eyes lifted. 'I'm not finding fault,' she confessed huskily. 'And how can I be your fiercest critic—we've hardly spoken?' *Hardly spoken…and today you're in his bed!*

'You don't need to speak—you have very eloquent eyes. You have been hating me silently for two years. When I woke up this morning the last person I expected to end up in bed with was Samantha Maguire.' *Except in my dreams.* But a man wasn't responsible for what his subconscious got up to. 'Who did *you* expect to end up in bed with?'

His wicked grin flashed out, and Sam realised that she didn't want to do this with anyone else. It was a revelation she had to share. 'I only want you.'

He laced his long brown fingers into her damp hair and pressed his lips to the pulse-point at the base of her neck. By the time he reached her mouth she was writhing with pleasure. 'I like a woman who knows what she wants.'

As they lay side by side on the bed she slowly ran her fingers over the long white scar that ran the length of his flank, and then over the network of smaller scars above his knee. 'I had no idea you were hurt so badly, Alessandro,' she said huskily.

'It looks worse than it was,' he lied, catching her hand and bringing it to his mouth.

Accepting that he didn't want to talk about it, she sighed with pleasure as his hand curved over her bottom. Lifting her mouth from his some time later, she touched a finger to the scar just below the hem of the silk boxers he wore. 'Does it go all the way?'

He smiled that stunning, wicked smile that made her heart flip and husked, 'No, *cara*, but I do.' Laughing at her blushes, he tipped her onto her back with masterful expertise and reached for the tie of her robe.

Before he slid the knot, she grabbed his hand in both of hers. 'I'm not very…'

Gently but firmly he took her hands, one by one, curving her fingers around the metal bedframe. 'I think we should have no secrets, *cara*.'

Sam held onto the bedframe for dear life and closed her eyes, sure that the moment he unwrapped her he might change his mind. 'No…' he cautioned, kissing her eyelids. 'Open your eyes.'

Her breath coming in short, painful bursts, Sam did as he requested. 'I…can't…'

'Relax…'

Relax! She was in bed with the most beautiful man she had ever seen, who happened to be half naked and about to undress her. In other circumstances she might have laughed. At that moment holding her breath seemed a more appropriate response.

Slowly, his eyes holding hers, he unslid the knot on her robe and parted the fabric. Alessandro swallowed before his eyes dropped.

A reverent cry of, '*Dio*, but you are perfect!' was torn from his lips.

Sam sagged with relief, then tensed again as his hand closed over first one taut tender breast and then the other, stroking her skin, teasing the straining, prominent peaks to new heights of quivering pleasure with his fingers and then his lips.

She snaked her fingers into his dark hair and said his name, her voice aching with the same inarticulate longing that drenched her body. To see his dark head against her pale skin was so unbelievably erotic that Sam writhed and arched her back, pushing up against him, gasping a little as their naked bodies touched, and then a lot more when his hand slid down the length of her smooth pale thigh.

Levering himself up until his face was level with hers, he looked deep into her eyes before he kissed her, and Sam clutched at him, her fingers digging into the taut golden flesh of his back as she moaned, *'Please…'* into his mouth.

She had no idea what she needed, but Alessandro was not similarly inhibited. He seemed to know where she wanted to be touched before she did! As his skilful mouth and hands moved over her body she gave a fractured groan and called out his name again, almost sobbing with the strength of her desire.

Sam had no idea how long he touched her any more than she had any idea of at what point she lost her inhibitions about him exploring every intimate part of her. Or being bold about doing the same to him. But when Alessandro finally pulled her beneath him and moved over her she was ready for the next step.

Actually, she was begging for his sensual invasion!

Her body tensed for a moment as he slid into her. Above her she was aware of his doing the same thing. For a moment neither of them moved.

Sam closed her eyes and heard his shocked inhalation, felt his breath warm on her cheek and neck. 'Just go with it, *cara*.' The sensual rasp of his thickened voice was like a caress. 'I will

look after you. You don't have to stay in control. Trust me…just
let go…' he urged, sliding his hands under her bottom.

Of all the unexpected things that had happened to her that
day, this was perhaps the most unexpected. Sam found she did.
She *did* trust him. *Totally.* He was the most dangerous thing
that had ever happened to her, but she trusted him to keep her
safe. It made no sense, but it was incredibly liberating.

As the tension slid from Sam an exultant sigh shuddered
through her stretched body.

'You feel incredible,' she moaned, grabbing his tight but-
tocks because she felt as if she was falling. 'I can feel all of…'
A fractured moan was wrenched from her throat.

'So good at this…so beautiful…so tight…' As he moved
slowly, hot and hard inside her, sliding deeper and deeper, she
was aware of him in every individual tingling nerve-ending.
And as he moved he wasn't just inside her body, he was inside
her head. With each thrust and stroke he seeped into her senses.

Alessandro was part of her.

As the rhythm inside her built Sam said some wild things
that she shouldn't have—things concerning his complete and
total perfection, things about wanting him to do this to her for
ever and ever—but he said some pretty crazy things too.

'Now, just let go…!'

She did.

As her heart-rate returned to something approaching normal she gave a languid sigh. Alessandro's leg remained
thrown across her, pinning her to the bed—not that she felt
any urge to move from where she was. Her body was still
rocked with tiny golden aftershocks.

She stroked his dark head where it lay on the pillow and
smiled a sleepy, smugly contented smile. Her back arched a
little as he stroked a brown finger down the valley between
her pink-tipped breasts.

His dark lashes lifted from the sharp angle of his cheekbones. 'Why didn't you tell me…?'

Sam, who knew exactly what he was saying, closed her eyes and feigned innocence. 'Tell you what?'

'You have never been with a man, *cara*.'

'I was hoping you wouldn't notice.' She opened her eyes and saw no answering smile on his face. 'Sorry if I was totally clueless, but…' She reached up and stroked his lean cheek, feeling the first stirrings of reawakened sexual interest as she recalled the abrasive sensation of his stubble on her burning skin as he worked his way down her body. 'If you're willing to bear with me, I think I could be a very fast learner.' Then, realising that she was making a lot of assumptions she had no right to make she added quickly, 'Always supposing we ever…you…we decide…' Maybe he was already regretting it? Maybe he was wondering how to tell her she'd have to find someone else for lesson two?

'Perhaps we should get out our diaries and see if we have a spare afternoon?' he inserted, sounding unaccountably angry.

'I don't have a diary.' She held her breath, thinking, That's his cue to say, *And I don't have a spare afternoon.*

He didn't.

'You should have told me…'

'Are you angry?' She looked at his face, memorising each plane and angle. 'About the virgin stuff?'

The awkward addition made his lips quiver. 'I'm not angry. I'm…I would have been gentler…'

'That would have been a pity.' She laid her head on his chest and felt the vibration of his surprised laugh.

'Today was a first for us both.'

She lifted her head. 'It was?'

'I've never slept with a virgin before. The women I—'

'I know,' she said quickly. 'They're like you. That's the way *I* want to be,' she told him, thinking, *I can do this!* 'If you want me, that is…' She swallowed, trying and failing to read his expression.

'*If I want you…?*' he echoed, sounding really strange. He

rolled onto his back. She watched as he lifted a hand and then just lay there.

Sam stared at his chest, rising and falling. His hand fell away, and as he turned his head towards her she held her breath.

'Oh, I want you,' he said thickly, and as he reached for her with a sigh of relief she went to him.

Much later, when the room had grown dark, Alessandro got up from the bed to throw a log on the dying embers of the fire. His tall, lean body was silhouetted against the dancing flames as he walked back to the bed.

My God, he's so beautiful!

'A fire in the bedroom is very…decadent,' she murmured as she snuggled up to him.

Alessandro ran a finger down the supple curve of her spine, and in the dark she smiled.

Her smile guttered when he asked quietly, 'Should we be worried?'

Sam knew immediately what he was talking about. The second time they had made love she had not known what he was apologising for until he had explained that the condom had broken. Still floating on a blissful cloud after their slow, sensuous, mind-blowing lovemaking, the implications of his explanation had not hit her. Now they did.

She did some speedy mental calculations and shook her head. 'No, it'll be fine,' she said, with more confidence than she actually felt.

'Well, you would tell me if…?'

Sam frowned. 'I told you—it'll be fine. I'm so glad I set-tled…'

His finger stopped stroking, but stayed where it was.

'Settled…?'

'Uh-huh,' she confirmed sleepily. Passion expended an awful lot of energy. 'My mum is always saying there's no point waiting for Mr Perfect because he doesn't exist…you should settle…'

'But he *does* exist, doesn't he?'

Bewildered by the edgy note that had entered his deep voice, Sam turned her head on the pillow, and in the shadows found his taut expression inexplicably hostile. 'What do you mean?'

'I mean Jonny was your Mr Perfect, and as he was unavailable you *settled* for me. It is not flattering for a man to realise the woman in his arms was thinking of another man while he made love to her. *Madre di Dio,* do you think I will tolerate being someone you *settle* for?'

'Thinking about someone else…?' she parroted, as though the words had no meaning. Which, of course, they didn't. With her body and mind drenched down to cellular level with awareness of Alessandro, Sam was having understandable trouble getting her head around this idea.

She met his suspicious, angry eyes and experienced a blinding flash of comprehension and anger.

'For goodness' sake, I couldn't even remember my own name—couldn't figure out where you ended and I started. *Think about someone else?*' she ejaculated with a bitter laugh. 'You're the last man in the world I'd have thought needed his ego massaging. Surely someone has mentioned before now the fact that you're really very, *very* good at this?'

'*Dio!*' he breathed as, overcome by embarrassment, she buried her face in his chest. 'I really never know what you're going to say next.'

She slid her hands over the soft whirls of dark hair on his chest and ran a finger across his masculine nipple. 'Neither do I.'

The husky admission drew a short laugh from Alessandro, who placed a hand underneath her bottom and scooped her towards him.

'When my mum was saying all that stuff about Mr Perfect I was still thinking in terms of a life partner. Now I realise I'm not actually suited to marriage.'

'You're not…?'

She shook her head emphatically. The last thing Alessandro wanted was a clingy, needy woman. 'No—definitely not. I'm too selfish. I like my life the way it is…' Her eyelashes swept downwards as she added huskily, 'With certain additions.'

He rolled over until he was looking down into her face and her body was pinioned by his long, lean length. 'A lover being one of those *certain additions*…?'

Not just *any* lover. Her perfect lover.

She nodded. 'Nobody needs to know—I mean, it's not as if we would be dating, or a couple or anything. We'd just be…' She felt the heat run up under her skin as, trying to sound nonchalant, she finished, *'This.'*

'You want this to be a secret affair?'

He looked shocked—or was that relieved? 'Not secret, exactly, but…'

'You don't want to broadcast it?'

'It'll be a lot simpler that way,' she observed, saying what she thought he wanted to hear. If giving him space was the only way to keep him, she could do it, she told herself.

There was a long pause before he said, 'I'm all for a simple life.'

'I thought you would be.'

CHAPTER TEN

ALESSANDRO had been ripping off his clothes with flattering speed when she'd run, laughing, into the bathroom. She had called his name and got no response, and then waited, her heart pounding with anticipation. But when after several minutes the door to the shower cubicle remained closed Sam didn't linger. After shampooing her hair with unnecessary vigour she stepped out.

'Obviously I'm not as irresistible as I think,' she told her image in the steamy mirror. 'Oh, my, do I have a problem.'

Of course there was a problem—and it wasn't restricted to talking to herself! Casual she could do—casual was fine—but casual *wasn't* living for the brief moments they shared. It simply wasn't healthy when for most of the time she was just going through the motions, waiting for him to call or like tonight, ring her doorbell.

The fact was she wanted more, and more was something Alessandro didn't want to give. If he knew how she felt Sam suspected he would run a mile. There was a choice, of course. There was always a choice. She could come clean, tell him how she felt and watch him walk away. Or she could accept what she had.

What was called a lose-lose situation.

Wrapping a towel sarong-wise around her still damp body, Sam stalked back into the bedroom. The first thing she saw was Alessandro. He was actually pretty hard to miss, standing in the middle of the room doing his dark, brooding stare thing into the middle distance.

Well, at least he hasn't fallen asleep, she thought as she walked straight past him and sat herself down at the dressing table. Maintaining a stony silence, she ostentatiously removed his jacket from the back of the chair and dropped it in an untidy heap on the floor. The provocation provoked no reaction. He just stood there, in the same state of semi-undress as he had been when she left.

But something had obviously occurred to put him in such a vile mood, since he had walked into the room looking at her as though she was water and he was a man who'd spent the last ten days walking through a desert.

She lifted a brush and then with a sigh set it down. 'Are you going to tell me what I'm supposed to have done now…?'

In the mirror their eyes clashed, stormy green with cold, implacable brown.

'Why do you assume you have done something?'

'Maybe something to do with the fact you could cut the atmosphere in here with a knife, but mostly because you've got your judge, jury and executioner face on,' she told him sweetly. 'You know, this makes me really sick,' she observed. 'I've waited an entire week for you to contact me.' *Which makes me the sort of pathetic idiot I swore I'd never be.* 'And now you are here all you can do is look at me as though I'm…'

'*Dio mio*, do not take that tone with me!' His unbuttoned shirt billowed as he strode across the room, revealing the sleek, toned lines of his bronzed torso. Taking hold of the back of her swivel chair, he stood there, glaring at her in the mirror.

Sam, who didn't have the faintest idea what was going on, glared right back.

'If you don't like it you know what you can do!' The least a part-time lover could do was be civil when he did deign to put in an appearance. This no-strings, no-explanation thing sounded great in theory, and maybe it worked for some people, but Sam had come to appreciate that she wasn't one of them.

If I had an ounce of guts I'd tell him it's over. Only where Alessandro was concerned she had the backbone and moral fibre of an invertebrate. How many times had she seen and silently sneered at friends who were willing to make concession after concession for their boyfriends? *I'd never do that,* she had thought, from her position of moral superiority. *And look at me now!*

'Don't think I won't.'

Empty threats…is this what I've been reduced to…?

'Good!' she snapped, thinking, I might be able to do better than 'good' if I had the faintest idea what we were fighting about.

'I suppose you have a perfectly reasonable explanation for this?'

As he bent across her the scent of his warm body caused Sam's nostrils to flare. 'What…?' she said, picking up the creased piece of paper he had slammed down on the dressing table. Her eyes widened as she recognised Jonny's cheque, which she had shoved in her bag and forgotten about.

'What is that?'

'A cheque.'

A harsh expletive was torn from Alessandro's throat. 'I know it's a cheque,' he growled. 'Do not be evasive.' His dark, angry eyes glared back at her from the mirror.

Sam, who had Jonny's secret to guard, had every intention of being evasive for as long as she could—although the expression on Alessandro's face suggested that wouldn't be very long.

She shrugged. 'If you know, why ask?'

His lean face was drawn into savage lines of anger as he spun her chair around and, curving his big body towards her, planted a hand on either arm.

Sam's eyes lifted as his shadow fell across her.

'A cheque for a large amount of money, made out to you,

from my sister's husband. What is Jonny doing, giving you money?' he demanded in a low, driven voice.

'Are you trying to intimidate me…?' If I had any sense at all, she thought, he'd be succeeding. It was pretty obvious from the scorching anger etched into every glorious line of his incredible face that he was just about combustible!

'I am trying to extract a straight answer from you,' he gritted back grimly.

'What were you doing going through my bag?'

He looked outraged at the suggestion. 'I wasn't. The damned thing was sitting there on the bedside table. It fell on the floor, I picked it up and…' He stopped, the muscles of his brown throat visibly working as he recalled the moment when he had realised what he held in his hand. 'What is Jonny doing giving you money, Samantha?'

Sam shrugged, his judgemental attitude causing her to respond with more provocation than was probably sensible. But actually she didn't feel sensible. She felt absolutely fed up that he so obviously didn't trust her. The injustice of it made her want to scream.

'I don't owe you any explanations, Alessandro.' He had certainly never offered *her* any, she thought resentfully. 'You're my lover, not my keeper, and that,' she warned him, 'could change at any moment. And anyway,' she added, 'it wasn't a gift, it was a loan.'

The semantics caused his lips to spasm derisively. 'You will not take money from another man.'

'I did n—' She stopped, her eyes narrowing. 'Another man? Does that mean *you're* offering?'

'Would that not smack of payment for services rendered?'

There was no pause for thought between the intention and the action. Her arm went back in a curve, released, and her hand made contact with his cheek. Alessandro, a look of stark incredulity on his face, straightened up, breathing hard.

Shaking, Sam too scrambled to her feet, pushing her chair

backwards against the dressing table. 'Look what you made me do!' she accused, appalled by her own actions.

'I *made* you?'

'Yes, you made me!' she yelled back. 'You, with your nasty insinuations and always believing the worst.'

'Are you going to tell me what that money is for?'

Sam shook her head, her expression blank. 'No, I'm not.'

'No problem. I will ask Jonny.'

Panic flared in Sam's eyes. 'You can't do that!' she protested.

'You leave me no choice.'

Sam closed her eyes and shook her head. 'My God, but I hate you!'

His lips curled into a sardonic half-smile. 'At this moment,' he confided, 'I'm not particularly fond of you.' But he still wanted to unwind that towel and throw her on the bed. He wanted it so badly he could taste it.

Slinging him a look of loathing, Sam walked across to the bed and sat down before her shaking legs gave way. 'I haven't cashed the cheque, and if you'd bothered to read the date you'd have noticed that's it's almost two months old.'

Alessandro's dark brows drew together in a straight line. 'So why haven't you cashed it?'

'I couldn't stop him giving it to me, but I didn't have to cash it.'

'Do men often feel driven to give you large amounts of money?' At that moment *he* felt driven—*very* driven. The fact that even at this moment all he could think of was burying himself deep inside her and hearing her say, *Yes, Alessandro,* in that breathy little voice that killed his much vaunted self-control stone-dead, was some measure of the spell she exerted over him.

Face facts, Alessandro, his inner voice goaded contemptuously. While you're desperately trying to act as if nothing has changed, the fact is *everything* has changed. You're *so* in control you felt it necessary to sweat for twenty-four hours just to prove that you didn't have to get off the plane and rush to the side of a woman who hasn't made any effort to contact you.

Sam, realising that she had no option but to tell him the truth and hope he kept it to himself, sighed and said, 'Jonny wasn't giving it to me. He was paying me back.' She looked at Alessandro, who just stood there, giving the impression he wasn't even listening. 'Did you hear what I said?'

Alessandro released a long pent-up breath and looked at her. 'No…yes.' A frown formed on his lean face. *'Paying you back…?'*

'Jonny had some cashflow problems and I lent him a little to tide him over until he sorted himself out.'

One dark brow elevated. 'A *little*…?' he said, picking up the cheque and waving it under her nose. 'You think that is a little…?'

Sam flushed under his ironic gaze. 'Well, it was only sitting in my account.'

'I'm all for making your money work for you, but you didn't choose the safest form of investment, did you? At least I know now why he hasn't been to me…'

'You're the last person he'd go to.'

Alessandro's dark lashes lifted from the high angle of his cheekbones. 'And you are the first, it seems,' he slotted in drily.

'Well, at least I don't make him feel inadequate,' she retorted. 'I think you enjoy intimidating people,' she accused.

Alessandro raised an arm to drag a frustrated hand through his dark hair. The rippling this action set in motion over his lean torso caused her to lose the thread of her argument.

'He should have gone to his wife, not to another woman,' Alessandro condemned. 'And the fact is lending him money is only delaying the inevitable.'

Sam, her colour heightened, wrenched her fascinated gaze from his body and said angrily, 'I am not *another* woman.'

'You are not *his* woman.' *You're mine!*

'But I am his friend, and with a brother-in-law like you, boy, does he need one! For God's sake, Alessandro, why can't you give the man a chance? So he's no financial genius…' She lifted her shoulders in an expressive shrug. 'So what? He's doing his best. And no man could love your sister more than he does.'

Alessandro's eyes dropped to where her heaving bosom was on the point of escaping the confines of the towel. 'Would you defend *me* with so much passion?' he wondered, lifting his gaze to her face .

'Defend you…?' she parroted, and laughed. 'What do you need defending against?' she wondered. 'You're so tough you're virtually bullet-proof,' she accused.

The streaks of colour emphasising the strong, carved contours of his cheekbones deepened as he responded in a voice that leaked derisive scorn, 'I would certainly not beg money from a woman.'

'He didn't beg!' Sam protested. 'I found out by accident.'

'Accident…?'

'Yes, *accident*.'

'You mean he was drunk?'

Sam read the contemptuous condemnation in the lean, starkly beautiful contours of his face and her lips tightened. 'Small wonder Jonny didn't want to come to *you* for help.'

'I imagine he knew that I would not hand him a blank cheque and offer him tea and sympathy.' He flashed her a cold smile. 'Or was it hugs and kisses?'

'He doesn't want my hugs and kisses.'

Alessandro looked at her mouth, so soft, lush and inviting, and wondered how any man worthy of the name could not want to enjoy them. If Jonny wanted to keep his teeth intact he'd better carry on *not* wanting, he mused grimly. If he had suspected for one second that Jonny harboured any inappropriate feelings for Samantha he would already have taken action.

'Presumably if he did you would not be in my bed.'

She looked at his mouth, thought about it on her skin, and thought, I would be in your bed if I had to crawl there! 'I'm not in *your* bed.'

Alessandro's eyes slid from hers as Sam followed the direction of his gaze to the tumbled quilt she had hastily pulled across the bed when she had realised who was ringing the doorbell. The colour flew to her cheeks.

His voice dropped to a sexy rasp. 'That could easily be fixed.' He accompanied this with the sort of raw, hungry look that stripped her nerve-endings bare and caused goosebumps to break out like a rash on her overheated skin.

Making contact with the sizzling heat in his sensational eyes, she felt her anger and resistance melting faster than snow in July. Gritting her teeth, she clung to the last shreds of her resentment, reminding herself that this relationship was too one-sided.

'That's *my* bed.'

'Does it matter whose bed it is?' Alessandro responded impatiently—because he could think of very little else but her legs wrapped around him as she lay soft and warm beneath him…or maybe on top…?

'I've never been in *your* bed.' Sam's voice went cold as she added bitterly, 'I've never been in your bedroom, or even in your home.'

Alessandro had been scrupulously careful to keep her well away from anyone who knew him. She didn't even know the location of his London home.

'Which is fine by me,' she assured him breezily. 'I wouldn't want to meet any of your friends.' And it was painfully obvious he didn't want any of them meeting his *bit on the side*.

Alessandro looked disconcerted by the acrid observation. 'What are you talking about?'

Meet his friends…? Their casual arrangement, which he was finding increasingly unsatisfactory, meant they spent precious little time together as it was. Having his friends monopolise her time? Sure, he was *really* going to do that!

'I'd probably have as little in common with them as I do you.'

The stubborn, tight-lipped contention caused his taut jaw to tighten another notch. 'You have met Smithie.'

Sam's expression softened slightly as she thought of Alessandro's ex-nanny. 'But she's not like your other friends.'

He raised an eloquent brow. 'As you have never met them, how would you know what my friends are like?'

Sam's eyes narrowed with dislike on his lean face. 'Not *everyone* considers me such a social liability.'

'Social liability...!' he echoed. 'Why do you insist on putting words in my mouth?'

'I don't!' she protested mutinously. 'It's *obviously* what you're thinking.'

A hissing sound of frustration escaped through his clenched teeth. *'Fine!'* he said, flinging up his hands in a very Latin gesture of irritation. 'I will arrange a dinner...no, I will arrange a *reception,* and introduce you to everyone I know. Will you be happy then? Or would you like me to invite a camera crew from one of those magazines that specialise in glossy spreads of such things into my home? We can be pictured lounging beside the pool and gush about how inseparable we are...will *that* make you happy?'

His biting sarcasm stung. 'It would make me sick.'

'Then, you see, we *do* have something in common after all. I value my privacy, and I thought you felt the same way.'

What he valued was his freedom. 'Don't glower at me that way. I'm not Jonny.'

His expression darkened. 'You know, I am sick of the sound of that name.' An expression of brooding discontent settled on his lean features as he thought about the younger man. 'I still don't understand why, if he needed money, he didn't come to me?'

'You are Kat's brother—the poor, deluded girl thinks

you're perfect… Jonny is afraid he'll look a wimp by comparison with her *marvellous* brother.' Her expression left no doubt that she didn't share the younger girl's opinion.

'Nonsense!'

The way he brushed aside her explanation made Sam's general crankiness morph into genuine anger. 'That's *so* typical of you. If you don't want to hear something you just pretend it isn't so. But ignoring it doesn't make it any less the truth. The truth is you make Jonny feel incompetent and second best.'

'He *is* incompetent, and also boring—I have no wish to talk about him any longer.' If he didn't get her into bed some time in the next ten seconds he was going to lose his mind…although it was always possible he had already lost it. A swift mental review of his recent behaviour brought a self-derisive twist to Alessandro's lips.

Sam flung up her hands. 'See—you can't help yourself!' she exclaimed.

Alessandro remained unmoved by her dramatic hand-waving. 'I thought you set great store by honesty?' But then I used to think the same about myself, he thought, considering his recent self-deception.

Damn the man—he always had an answer. 'So, if he *had* come to you, what would you have done…?'

'That depends. But I certainly wouldn't have thrown good money after bad.'

'You'd have let him go under?' she accused, shocked by his unapologetic admission. 'But that amount of money is absolutely nothing to you!' she protested, clicking her fingers to underline her point. 'My God, Alessandro, you're so callous.'

'I'd have told him to cut his losses and find something he wants to do. He is clearly doing something he neither enjoys or is suited to. I would have told him to find something he can be passionate about.'

'You make it sound so easy, but Jonny isn't like you…'

His jaw clenched. 'You wish me to emulate your hero…?'

'There's no need to be stupid. Jonny is not my hero.'

Something flickered at the back of his dark eyes. There was a short, dense silence before he added huskily, 'And am I?'

The question threw Sam totally off her stride. 'Stupid? Or my hero…?' She angled an uncertain look at his face and discovered nothing from his shuttered expression. Did he want to be her hero? It seemed pretty unlikely.

'My hero would display a little bit of faith in me—not to mention have some respect for my views,' she retorted, avoiding a direct answer. 'But actually I don't think I need a hero. Actually, I don't think I need a lover.'

If the moment of shocked silence that followed her announcement had lasted another micro-second longer Sam would have retracted it. Only it didn't.

'You wish me to leave?'

Of course it might have been possible to retract her reckless words even then, if he had acted for a moment as if he gave a damn one way or the other. But he just stood there, looking remote in the way only he could, so she dug herself a little deeper and said, 'Well, there doesn't seem much point in you staying, does there?'

'I will not impose on you any longer,' he said, looking so stiff and starchy she almost expected him to click his heels!

She felt numb with shock and disbelief as he walked out of the door, but still managed to scream a defiant, 'Good riddance!' at the top of her lungs, before bursting into noisy, emotional sobs.

She eventually convinced herself that she was better off without him.

It took her twelve hours of intermittent weeping and numerous attempts to trivialise her feelings for Alessandro to arrive at this conclusion, but when she got there she knew it was a plateau—a point from which her life could move on in an

infinitely saner and more productive direction. It was, she told
herself, good that things had come to a head when they had.
It wasn't as if she had ever thought the relationship had staying power.

After all, she was far too old to believe in fairy tales, and
if the last few weeks had taught her anything they had taught
her that she didn't want a life fraught with dramatic ups and
downs. It might suit some people, but she liked an ordered,
organised existence, and she was looking forward to things
getting back to normal.

Of course at that point Sam didn't realize that *normal* had
vanished for ever. That happened a week later.

CHAPTER ELEVEN

DOOR keys held in her teeth, one bag balanced on her hip, a sheaf of property leaflets under her arm and two bags of groceries gradually cutting off the circulation to her fingers, Sam climbed the stairs to her second-floor flat. There were many plus points about living on the second floor of this tasteful Edwardian conversion, including a lovely view of the park, but carrying her weekly groceries upstairs was not one of them.

The impossibility of ferrying groceries, a buggy and a baby was one of the reasons she had done a trawl of the local estate agents after she'd waved goodbye to her mother.

God knew how her mother had guessed, but at least she had been spared finding the right moment to tell her parents. She was pretty sure that, despite her mother's solemn promise not to tell her father yet, it wouldn't be long before he also knew.

Her mother always meant it when she said conspiratorially, *We won't tell your father about this, Sam.* But it didn't really matter if *this* was the price of a new pair of shoes or a dent in the new car, the moment George Maguire walked through the door she blurted out the truth. Not only was she incapable of keeping a secret from her husband, she appeared blind to this defect in her character.

Sam had dropped the bags and retrieved the keys from her mouth before she realised she had a visitor.

'I have been waiting for an hour.'

The breath left her lungs in one gasp as she spun around. Stunned to silence, she just stared. Alessandro, minus his suit but complete with the restless vitality she would always associate with him, stood there. His long legs sheathed in a pair of faded denims, he slouched elegantly, one ankle crossed over the other and his broad shoulders wedged against the wall of the hallway she shared with the other top floor flat.

As she stared, her emotions a turbulent cocktail of longing and loathing, he levered himself off the wall. The black designer T-shirt he wore was fitted enough to allow her to see the tightening of the muscles in his flat belly… She blinked hard to banish the image and bit down on her lower lip.

It had been three weeks since she had last seen him, and she had counted every second.

'You…here…' As if there was any doubt about it! The touch of his dark compelling eyes, the scent of his body… God, who else *but* Alessandro could reduce her to a mindless bundle of hormonal craving by his mere presence?

What was more to the point was *why*?

He arched a brow and looked her up and down. 'You were expecting someone else?'

Failing miserably to adopt the desired attitude of defiance to mask her real feelings, Sam mutely shook her head. Hands clenched into tight balls, she didn't even notice the pain as her nails dug into the flesh of her palms. This, she decided, was the substance of nightmares. Thinking of nightmares turned her thoughts to the frequent occasions when he had featured in her more torrid nocturnal dreams. A rush of shamed heat slammed through her body.

'You're here…'

'We have covered that,' he said, making no attempt to conceal his growing impatience.

'Well, why…?'

'Yes, I am here…for an hour I have been here.' His narrow-eyed, disapproving glance roamed hungrily over her slender body. His manner was terse and impatient as he looked down his patrician nose and demanded, 'Where the hell have you been?'

The flight back from New York had begun productively enough. He had been working his way through the pile of paperwork he had brought with him with his usual methodical speed. Then, somewhere mid-Atlantic, he had allowed the infuriating redhead to creep insidiously into his head. She was on another continent, she was a distraction—yet his body had responded to the imaginary scent of her warm body in his nostrils.

Suddenly not being the one to make the first move had seemed less a matter of principle and more an action of wilful stupidity. What was he trying to prove anyway? It wasn't as if he had any illusions about the nature of his true feelings. The realisation hadn't been a bolt from the blue, but gradually it had crept up on him—he didn't want a casual relationship!

He didn't want some secret little affair.

He wanted Samantha. And he wanted the world, and especially anyone called Jonny Trelevan, to know that she was his.

Putting aside the papers, he'd pulled out the small box secreted in his inside pocket. His expression distant and unfocused, he'd been staring at the square-cut emerald when a passing flight attendant, who had been about to ask him if he required anything, had released a soft, awed cry.

Alessandro had lifted his head.

The girl had flushed a little and given an apologetic shrug. 'Sorry—it's just beautiful. The colour is so intense,' she'd observed, her envious glance drifting to the ring lying on its ruched bed of velvet. Unable to hide her curiosity, she'd added. 'She must be someone very special…?'

Alessandro, his eyes trained on the ring, had nodded. 'She is. But she is also as stubborn as hell. But you know something…? I wouldn't have her any other way.'

The reflective smile that had curved his sensual lips upwards had dimmed as he became aware of the attendant's amazed stare. Shoving the box back into his pocket, he'd announced that he did not require anything.

And why wouldn't she stare…? he'd mused as she left—no doubt to spread the story. A man famed for his ability to cut dead anyone unwise enough to delve into his personal life had gushed on like something straight out of a women's magazine.

He had played out various versions of this scene, where she'd open the door and find him standing there, during the remainder of the journey—while the paperwork had lain untouched. She would, of course, regret her previous unreasonable behaviour, and he in his turn would magnanimously forgive her before he proposed.

In none of those versions had there been no response. In none of those versions had there been three day's worth of newspapers protruding from her letterbox.

A rush of anger enabled Sam to regain the power of speech. 'And that would be any of your business because…?' She angled an ironic brow and, looking at his face, felt a wave of longing so intense, so *visceral*, that for a moment she stopped breathing. 'Of course if I'd known I was meant to be on twenty-four-hour call just in case you decided to *honour* me with your presence I would naturally have stayed home.'

'There were three days' newspapers stuck in the door.' He brandished the offending items, which were barely recognisable as such now, after being slapped repeatedly against his thigh as he paced up and down.

'An open invitation to burglars and one would have thought a cause of concern for your neighbours…' His lips twisted contemptuously as he added drily, 'Though apparently not.' The shifty-looking type in the flat across the corridor had shrugged and looked uninterested when Alessandro had asked him if he knew when Miss Maguire would be home.

'Not the faintest, mate.'

'You are aware that there are three days' newspapers in the door?'

'If you say so… I wouldn't know.'

'And you wouldn't know or, I suppose, care if she was lying ill inside, would you?'

'I keep myself to myself. I don't want any trouble.'

Sam tucked her hair behind her ears and gave a shrug. 'I must have forgotten to cancel them.'

This casual admission caused his jaw to tighten. 'You could have been inside…' The muscles in his brown throat worked as his eyes slid from hers. *'Hurt…'*

'If you were so worried I'm surprised you didn't call the police,' she countered, unable to believe he had been genuinely concerned for her safety. Much more likely he resented being kept waiting—which brought her back to the puzzling question of why he was here at all.

'I considered that, but I decided on reflection that it would be quicker to take a look…'

Sam shook her head, her smooth brow puckered. 'Take a look? What do you mean—?' She stopped, an expression of horror crossing her face as she looked from him to her front door. Ignoring the key in her hand, she pushed the door. It immediately swung inwards.

'I don't believe it—you broke into my flat…you broke in! How could you…?'

'It was not difficult. The security in this building is appalling.'

She swung back, her eyes flashing. 'Don't get smart with me!' she recommended grimly.

Alessandro picked up the grocery bag she had dropped on the floor and walked past her into the flat. 'I think you are making too much of this. I was concerned…'

'Concerned! Nosy, more like. How would *you* like your privacy being invaded? How would you like someone going through your drawers?'

'Relax—your secrets are safe. I prefer your underwear with you in it.'

Sam drew a startled breath as her aquamarine eyes lifted to his. A shock of white-hot excitement washed over her, infiltrating every individual Alessandro-deprived cell of her body as their glances connected.

'Save the smouldering looks, Alessandro,' she growled angrily. 'They don't do a thing for me,' she lied.

'You are a terrible liar, *cara.*'

'Oh, God!' she groaned, lifting a hand to her cheek. 'Don't do this to me, Alessandro.'

'What am I doing to you, *tesoro mio*?'

Appalled, because his chest was the only place her head wanted to be, Sam walked over to the window and lifted the casement. Ducking her head outside, she took several restorative gulps. She tensed and closed her eyes as she sensed him come up behind her. When his hands came to rest on her hips instinct took over and she leaned back into him with a sigh.

It was the sound of crunching metal that broke the spell.

'What was that?' Alessandro, his expression curious, but at that point unalarmed, leaned past her to see through the window. 'That woman has driven straight into my car.'

'"That woman" is my mother.'

'Your mother!' He winced, as there was a further agonised crunching of metal as the Volvo reversed away from the rear of his gleaming Mercedes.

'She says that's what bumpers are for,' Sam explained, as her parents emerged from the Volvo and her mother's voice drifted upwards.

'I thought there was plenty of space, George.'

'Let me do the talking…'

Sam closed her eyes and covered her face with her hands. She had long ago come to the conclusion that her parents' main objective in life was to embarrass her as much as was possible. But today they were surpassing themselves.

'My car…'

Sam's hands fell away from her face. 'Never mind your stupid car,' she hissed. If dented cars were the worst thing to come out of this she would consider herself very lucky indeed. Being a realist, she knew this was unlikely.

This slight made him look offended. 'My *stupid* car…?'

'Well, it's only a car, and I'm sure you have dozens of others. My parents are coming up…'

'And you want me not to mention your mother's driving?'

'I want you not to be here.' Her sinking heart reached rock bottom. Short of making him climb down the drainpipe, she was going to have to explain him being in her flat to her parents. Even *her* fertile imagination wasn't that creative. 'They can't find you here.'

He arched a sardonic brow, a frown forming on his face as he recognised the extent of her agitation. 'Why can't they find me here?'

'Because they might think—' She stopped, her eyes sliding away from his. What was she meant to say? *They might think you're the father of my baby, and they'd be right.*

'That we are lovers?' Sam was unable to tear her eyes from the nerve that had begun to throb in his lean cheek. 'You are ashamed to have your parents know of our relationship?'

'And you on the other hand are ready to shout it from the rooftops…I *don't* think,' she drawled. 'We can't exactly say you just dropped by for a chat, can we?'

'Why not?'

She looked at him, exasperated. 'Because they know I can't stand you.'

'Do you often have sex with men you can't stand?'

'You were the first.'

'In more ways than one,' he observed soberly.

'Oh, for heaven's sake—I don't know why you're so hung up about this virginity thing!' she groaned in exasperation. 'It's not like I was waiting for you specifically or anything.'

'Maybe…' One dark brow arched as he scoured her resentful features. 'But I seem to recall you saying you were glad you *had* waited, and that it was me.'

'And I,' she countered flushing deeply, 'recall you saying a lot of things not to be taken literally either.'

His eyes narrowed as he folded his arms across his chest. 'Such as…?'

'Such as I'm beautiful and sexy and…' Her eyes slid from his bold, provocative stare. 'Stuff,' she added gruffly, 'like that.'

'And you do not feel sexy or beautiful?'

As if he didn't know he had the ability to make any woman feel that way. 'I am a realist.'

'Realist!' he flared. 'You are the most irrational, contradictory female I have ever encountered.'

'Don't you dare start with that *you're an irrational female* guff!' she warned.

He looked from her angry pink cheeks to her tightly clenched fists and heaving bosom and smiled. 'You're the soul of reason, *cara*—' He stopped suddenly, his frowning gaze lingering on her soft features. 'You know, you look different…'

First Mum, now Alessandro…What is it with me? Did someone stick an 'I'm pregnant' sticker on my forehead when I wasn't looking?

'Nobody could stay reasonable around you. And the way I recall it you weren't too anxious to have your precious friends know about our *relationship*.'

A spasm of annoyance crossed his lean features. 'It was you who seemed to get some sort of thrill from our relationship being illicit. I just went along with it.'

Sam stared at him. '*Me…?* You're suggesting…?' Feeling pushed into a corner, she gritted defensively, 'You don't care about me. We didn't have a relationship—we had sex!' she blurted, thinking, *Please say it meant more.*

Only he didn't. In fact nothing in his manner suggested it had meant more—apart from a strong desire to throttle her.

The anger that had flared in his dark eyes faded as he recognised the glitter of unshed tears in her eyes. 'Not enough sex.'

Sam fought the surge of debilitating weakness that followed his seductively soft complaint.

'I came here this evening to rectify that.'

She stared at him, unable to think. Her body was literally thrumming with desire. And then there was a loud knock on the door.

'Don't answer it.'

His compelling glance locked with hers.

If he had touched her then Sam knew she would have gone along with his suggestion… Heck, she'd have gone along with just about any suggestion he cared to make! But he didn't. He just stood there, looking explosive and impossibly sexy, while he waited for her to give in.

Someone outside leaned on the doorbell and didn't let go.

Sam shook her head and tried to think…but every attempt at rational thought got as far as Alessandro naked. 'God, what am I going to do with you…?' She thought of some things she could do with him and her focus slipped another fatal notch.

'You want me to hide under the bed, perhaps…?'

Sam greeted this sarcastic interjection with a genuine sigh of relief. 'Of course!' she exclaimed. 'Why didn't I think of that?'

Outrage and disbelief stamped on his patrician features, Alessandro stared at her. 'You are suggesting I hide under your bed?'

'Not *under* the bed, obviously.' A grin formed on her lips as she looked him up and down. 'You wouldn't fit.' *But with me he fits perfectly.*

In response to the hands she laid flat against his chest, and without taking his fascinated gaze from her face, Alessandro began to back towards the closed door of her bedroom.

'You wish me to hide from your parents?' he said, as if he couldn't quite believe that was what she was suggesting.

'That's the general idea.' When he didn't respond she opened the door and gave him a push. 'And whatever you do,' she added, pressing a finger to her lips, 'don't make a sound. I'll get rid of them as quickly as I can.'

Just as she closed the door the doorbell rang again. Sam took a deep breath and straightened her shoulders. Chin up, she walked to the door and opened it. *If that doorbell hadn't rung when it did I could be doing something very stupid.*

A certain lack of appreciation for her narrow escape was responsible for the cranky expression on her face when she pulled open the door.

'Where's the fire? Mum and Dad—what are you doing here?' She looked from one to the other, pretending surprise, as she added under her breath, 'As if I didn't know. I suppose you'd better come in,' she added ungraciously.

'Sorry, darling, but it just slipped out,' her mother murmured contritely as they stepped past her into the sunny room.

'And just as well it did,' her father observed. 'I'm only disappointed my daughter didn't feel able to tell me herself.'

Sam accepted this parental chastisement with a rueful, apologetic grimace.

'Am I such a terrible father?'

Sam repressed a groan. Her father yelling she could take; it was infinitely preferable to Dad taking the blame. 'Of course not, Dad. I just…'

'Now, what is this nonsense about the father not wanting to know? *Not wanting to know!*' he repeated, his face reddening. 'What sort of irresponsible loser would not want to know about his own child?' he demanded.

'Dad, no matter what I say, you're not going to like it.'

'You tell me who he is, Samantha, and I'll change his mind,' he predicted rubbing his hands in anticipation.

Sam's eyes flickered towards the bedroom door—her father's gruff voice had a penetrating quality and the walls of the flat were paper-thin. She guided them towards the kitchen area, which was farthest from the bedroom. 'Will you calm down, Dad?' she begged. 'It's not the end of the world,' she soothed.

'Calm!' George echoed in an incensed bellow that made Sam wince. 'My little girl gets pregnant by some loser,' he choked, 'and you expect me to stay calm!'

'Shall I open the window?' Sam enquired bitterly. 'I think that deaf lady in number three might not have heard you.'

Her father's eyes narrowed. 'This is no laughing matter. I'll wring the irresponsible bastard's neck. This guy is going to learn you don't mess with a Maguire.'

Sam rolled her eyes. 'You've been reading those Westerns again, haven't you, Dad?' She sighed. 'Say after me,' she suggested. 'I am not Wyatt Earp, I am a middle-aged GP who hates paperwork.' Her father did not return her coaxing smile, so with a rueful shrug she eased herself onto the countertop and began to swing her legs. Regressive behaviour she thought, and stopped swinging like the kid her father obviously considered her to be.

'You think this is some sort of joke, young lady?'

'No, Dad, I do not think this is some sort of joke. But I do think this is my life,' she said quietly. 'You have to let me do this my way.'

'Which is how?'

'I don't know yet,' she admitted.

Her father responded to this confession by pulling at his thinning sandy hair and groaning.

'I *knew* this was the way you'd react—which is why I asked Mum not to tell you. I'm not your little girl, Dad.'

'You'll always be my little girl.'

Sam, who was a whisker away from crying like a baby, sniffed loudly.

'Shall I make a nice cup of tea?'

Her husband and daughter turned to look at Ruth Maguire, their expressions both incredulous.

'*A nice cup of tea* isn't going to solve this, Ruth,' her husband informed her with withering scorn.

'Neither will wringing anyone's neck,' Sam pointed out. 'Actually, Mum,' she said, glancing at her watch, 'I need to be somewhere…'

'Well, if Sam needs to be somewhere, George—' Ruth began hopefully.

'I'm not going anywhere until I get some straight answers,' her husband announced bullishly. 'And neither are you, young…'

'You should have woken me, *cara*.' Rich and sleepily intimate, the deep voice cut across her father's irate rant.

CHAPTER TWELVE

WATCHING her father's jaw drop, Sam closed her eyes and felt her body flood with dread. Of course in hindsight she could see that this had been inevitable. You didn't shove a man with an ego like Alessandro's in a dark cupboard, or in this instance your bedroom, and *not* expect him to exact some sort of retribution.

Only he had not the faintest idea what he was walking into.

When she opened her eyes and turned her head she saw that Alessandro had pulled out all the stops. *I suppose*, she thought, swallowing past the aching constriction in her dry throat as her glance roamed hungrily across the expanse of rippling golden torso on show, *I should be grateful he kept his pants on!* Though the unbuckled belt that hung around his narrow hips and the unfastened top two buttons of his jeans were a nice touch, all geared to cause her the maximum embarrassment… My God, she thought, you have absolutely no idea of how embarrassing this is likely to get.

Barefooted, he padded into the room, moving with the inimitable sexy animal elegance that even at this moment she found totally riveting. 'Is that coffee I smell?'

No, it's fear, she thought.

Their eyes touched, and the malicious gleam in his told her that her reading of his motives had been bang on target. Still holding her eyes, he stretched lazily and lifted a hand to his artfully tousled sable hair. He stopped, and appeared to notice they were not alone.

An Oscar-winning performance, she mused, watching self-consciousness register on his face as he looked at her parents. *Self-conscious?* Sure, that was really likely, she thought struggling to contain her indignation. She was pretty sure that Alessandro could walk stark naked into a Women's Institute meeting and not blush!

'Mum, Dad—you know Alessandro, I believe?'

'What does this mean, Samantha?' demanded her father, looking from the tall, half-naked Italian to her daughter.

Her mother, who had been staring as the splendid bronzed figure emerged with a stunned expression, suddenly released a long sigh and smiled as things clicked into place.

'For goodness' sake, George, what do you think it means?' Sounding exasperated, she flashed her husband a look loaded with meaning. The smile she then bestowed on Alessandro was so warm and approving that he in his turn looked taken aback.

In response to the questioning glance he flashed Sam, she shrugged. He'll look even more taken aback once he realises that Mum is measuring him up as potential son-in-law material, Sam thought, swallowing the bubble of hysterical laughter that rose to her throat.

'You've been having an affair with this man?'

Sam flushed.

'Well?'

'Answer the man, *cara.*'

'Not an affair,' she snapped.

'He has just come out of your bedroom naked! What was he doing?'

'Well, why ask if you already know?'

Alessandro's dark brows drew together as he bared his teeth. 'Not an affair? Then what would your definition be?'

'The biggest mistake of my life!'

George, forgotten by the two combatants, went a shade

deeper and his barrel chest swelled with wrath as his glare moved from one to the other. 'You're not going to deny that you're sleeping with my daughter?'

'Of course he isn't. Now, please don't get excited, dear. It's bad for your blood pressure,' Ruth said, patting her husband's shoulder.

'I don't need you to tell me about my blood pressure—I'm a doctor!' George Maguire drew a deep breath and turned his narrowed gaze on the younger man. 'I want to know what you intend to do.'

'Putting on some clothes would be a good start—' Sam inserted drily, before Alessandro could respond to the challenge.

'Never mind that,' her father interrupted impatiently. 'What I want know is are you going to marry her?'

'*Marry!*' Alessandro exclaimed, looking shaken for the first time during this interchange.

'It hasn't even occurred to you, has it?' A look of contempt contorted the older man's face.

Sam closed her eyes and missed the revealing expression on Alessandro's face. She accepted that the point where she could avert disaster had passed, and held her breath and waited in a fatalistic fashion for the truth to emerge.

'Men like you are contemptible!' her father declared, looking at the younger man as though he was something unpleasant on his shoe. 'The scum of the earth.'

Alessandro's nostrils flared, his darkly defined brows lifted and his breathing quickened. But his expression remained politely enquiring, if slightly wooden. Sam thought that under the circumstances he was taking the scathing denouncement of his character quite well.

'I don't suppose this is the first time.'

'I am thirty-two, Dr Maguire.' Thirty-two, and I thought I would never find a woman I wanted to spend the rest of my life with. I finally do, and she is ashamed to acknowledge our relationship… Irony glittering in the dark depths, his eyes slid towards Sam as her father yelled.

'Is that meant to be funny? You obviously have no concept of decency whatsoever. Sam is right. She and the baby are better off without you.' Oblivious to the bombshell he had just delivered, George turned his attention to his daughter. 'I demand, Samantha, that you promise me here and now that you will never see this man again.'

'I'd not planned to,' she said, leaden as she looked into a future that held no Alessandro.

'*Baby…?*' The heel of his hand pressed to his forehead, Alessandro took his first breath for a full sixty seconds. His stunned dark glance swivelled back towards Sam.

Sam, thinking, *Here it comes,* watched the muscles in his brown throat working as he swallowed convulsively.

'*Baby…?*'

'This innocent act is all very well—' George began.

'Dad,' Sam interrupted, her eyes fixed on Alessandro's lean face. 'He didn't know.'

Her father gaped at her incredulously. 'You haven't told the man you're pregnant?'

Alessandro drew a deep, shuddering breath. '*Dio!*' His searing glance moved over Sam's flushed and defensive face before dropping to her stomach. 'You are pregnant?'

The focus of all eyes, Sam shrugged and pushed out her chin. 'Looks like it!'

'And I am the father…?' There were two slashes of dark colour along Alessandro's cheekbones as his eyes lifted to hers.

Sam took a deep, offended breath. 'It's possible,' she admitted between gritted teeth. 'But when double numbers are involved the maths get tricky.'

'Sam!' her mother reproached. 'She always gets flippant when she's embarrassed,' she explained in an aside to Alessandro.

Sam blinked furiously before the tears that filled her eyes

could fall. 'Thanks for the support, Mum, but I'm not embarrassed,' she muttered bitterly, before turning to the sink. She turned both taps on full blast and began to mechanically pile clean cups into the water.

'If you will excuse me, I need to have a private conversation with your daughter.'

Hands wet, Sam spun around. '*You* don't tell my parents to leave!' she snapped. 'The only person leaving here is you.'

'No, he's right, Sam. We should go. You have things to discuss.'

Sam stared at her father in amazement. 'What happened to *Promise me you'll never see this man again?*' she demanded.

'I didn't have the full facts,' her father retorted. He nodded towards Alessandro and cleared his throat. 'I might,' he conceded, 'have spoken out of turn.'

'You are a father. I would have reacted the same way in your place,' Alessandro said, taking the hand that was extended towards him.

Men…! Sam, watching the man-to-man handshake, was feeling nauseous. 'Sorry to interrupt this male bonding,' she gritted between clenched teeth. 'But actually you can *all* go!'

'Really, Sam,' her father reproved. 'Under the circumstances I think it's about time that you started showing a little maturity.' He turned to Alessandro. 'I can rely on you to do the right thing…?'

Alessandro, looking pale but composed, nodded. 'You can.'

Sam stood there in open-mouthed amazement as George guided his wife from the flat, pausing only to nod in a stomach-turning man-to-man way to Alessandro, who had apparently been transformed in his eyes from a defiler of innocence to a decent sort.

'Enjoy the warm approval while it lasts,' Sam suggested as the door closed. 'He won't be so keen on you once he realises that you're not about to marry me.'

Alessandro opened his mouth, then stopped and appeared

to change his mind about what he had been about to say. 'When were you going to tell me?' His lips twisted as their eyes connected. 'Or were you?'

Sam felt a guilty flush over her fair skin. 'Don't take that tone with me,' she snapped, reinserting her hands up to the elbows into soapy water.

Alessandro's narrowed eyes stayed on her slender back as she hunched over her diversionary chore. 'Well, were you?'

'Yes... No...' She drew a deep breath. 'Eventually, I suppose. I really don't see why you're making such a big thing of this.'

'You don't...?'

She flashed him an exasperated look over her shoulder and saw that his normally animated features were set in a stone-like mask. 'It's not like I'm asking you to support me or anything,' she pointed out reasonably. Maybe, she thought suddenly, he imagined she had ideas of using the baby to get her hands on some of his enormous fortune? Maybe, she speculated, going cold at the thought, it had crossed his mind that she'd got pregnant on purpose with that view in mind...?

'By most people's standards I make a pretty good living— very good, actually. There's no way I'll need any help financially... If you like, I'll sign something.'

'*Sign...?*'

Wiping her dripping hands on the legs of her jeans, she turned around, her expression earnest. 'To say I've got no claim whatsoever to your money just because of the baby. Honestly, I don't want a penny from you.' Her reassuring smile wobbled in the face of the murderous glare she got in response.

She found his response puzzling. He had a lot of money, by all accounts, but even very rich men, and it sometimes seemed to Sam even *especially* rich men, were notoriously reluctant to be parted from any of their cash. Maybe he hadn't understood what she was saying? She decided to spell it out.

'I'm not looking for any financial hand-outs.'

'You will sign something…?' A muscle in his jaw clenched as his eyes sealed with hers. 'You are talking about *money*?'

She nodded her head vigorously, to confirm the fact she had no avaricious expectations. 'That's right. You really shouldn't bother your head about this—it'll work out fine.' Sam wished that she was half as confident as she sounded. The truth was that, even putting to one side her concerns about the actual physical process of giving birth, the idea of having sole responsibility for another human being made her feel totally inadequate.

'So you have everything sorted?'

His tone made her flush. Did he think she didn't know that her life was about to change for ever?

'I'm aware that I'll have to make some adjustments—of course I am. And obviously I've not worked out all the details yet,' she admitted, skimming a defensive frown up at him. 'But I've only known a few weeks.'

The inarticulate sound that emerged from between Alessandro's clenched teeth stopped her dead.

'You have known a few weeks longer than I have.'

Observing for the first time the pallor that lent a grey tinge to his naturally vibrant skin tones, and the white line around his sensually sculpted lips, Sam's over-developed empathy sprang into painful life.

'I'm so sorry,' she said, her earnest tone filled with self-recrimination as she recalled the mind-numbing shock *she* had experienced when she had realised she was pregnant.

Alessandro looked startled. 'You are *sorry*?'

Not understanding the odd inflection in his voice, she nodded. Even a man as pragmatic and in control as Alessandro had a right to fall apart at a time like this. And Alessandro probably was the most in control sort of guy she had ever met. Except in bed. He was not always in control in bed. Without meaning to, she thought of skin against skin—which was a mistake, because wave after wave of scalding heat spilled through her body while the muscles in her abdomen went into painful spasm.

'Is something wrong?'

Tilting her head up to his, she lied smoothly through her fixed smile. 'I'm fine,' she said, rubbing her goosebump-covered forearms.

His narrowed eyes scanned her face. 'Well, you don't look it.'

'I don't enjoy scenes.'

'Then perhaps,' he counselled, 'you should not invite dramas.'

Sam took a deep, wrathful breath. 'Invite! I didn't invite anything—including you or my parents.' Her lower lip quivered. 'All I want is to be left alone.'

'Grow up, Sam.'

This piece of bracing advice brought a militant sparkle to her eyes. To be told twice in the space of an hour that she was being immature, and by men both times, was too much to take. '*You're* calling *me* childish…!' she exclaimed. 'And I suppose it was sophisticated and mature to strip off and come out of my bedroom that way?'

'I did not appreciate being treated like an embarrassment.'

'You were never keen to broadcast the fact we were lovers before.'

'I only ever went along with what *you* wanted…which was my first mistake,' he observed heavily.

What she wanted? That was rich. 'While you wanted to shout it from the rooftops, I suppose…?'

'Well, I did not want to creep around as though we were doing something to be ashamed of.'

'I wasn't ashamed. I knew you were—'

'I was what?' he prompted.

Sam shook her head. 'It doesn't matter.' Finding out he was going to be a father the way he had must, she realised with a fresh wave of empathy, have been like being hit over the head with a large blunt object.

'You're probably in denial…' The cat from next door jumped in at the open window and absently she reached out to stroke it.

'Denial?' His eyes flickered down as the cat brushed against his legs before disappearing under the sofa.

Her slender shoulders lifted. 'I was,' she admitted. But having your body change on an almost hourly basis was kind of hard to ignore even if you wanted to, and pretty quickly she had become fascinated with what was happening. How could she not? It was all a bit of a miracle…a scary miracle, maybe, but still a miracle.

Alessandro's head jerked up. Sam found his expression unsettling, but then she found most things about Alessandro unsettling. And on the bright side he had stopped looking at her as though she was demented—though she suspected this situation was temporary.

'When did you realise you were pregnant?'

Unconsciously she pressed a hand to her stomach and admitted huskily, 'I think I sort of knew straight off… When I couldn't put it off any longer I did a test…four tests, actually,' she corrected, recollecting with a wry smile her inability to believe the proof of her own eyes. 'This wasn't the way I intended to tell you… Not,' she added with a rueful burst of honesty, 'that I knew *what* I intended. I hadn't told anyone yet. My mother,' she added, anticipating his protest, 'guessed.'

'So I am not the last to know? I suppose that is something,' he conceded heavily.

'God,' she said, pushing the wispy curls of copper-coloured hair from her brow with the crook of her elbow, 'I could do with a cup of tea. Would you like one?' She motioned him to the sofa, and after a pause he lowered his tall, rangy frame onto the squashy cushions.

'I do not want tea.'

'I don't have anything stronger—except the cooking sherry I bought for trifle. I don't suppose you—?'

'No, I do not,' he confirmed. 'Why,' he wondered as she

began to dry the wet cups, 'do the British act as if a cup of tea is the answer to everything?'

'I presume the Italian way is to act as if sex is the answer to everything?' she countered crankily.

'There is certainly more room for creativity in making love than there is in dropping a teabag in a mug. And,' he added giving a wolfish grin, 'it lasts longer than tea.'

'If you do it properly,' she sniffed, feeling that familiar hot liquid quiver low in her belly.

A dark brow angled as he searched her face. 'Are you saying I don't…?'

The flush that she had so far kept at bay by sheer will-power spread up Sam's neck until her face was burning. 'You do it better than properly,' she admitted huskily. An image formed in her head and she added wistfully, 'You do it perfectly.' An impossible act to follow.

Without waiting to see how he'd reacted to this ill-judged piece of honesty, she reached into the fridge for milk.

'Leave that and come and talk to me.'

Sam straightened up. 'There's nothing to talk about. I have everything sorted.'

'You can't seriously believe that?'

'Would you prefer coffee—?'

'Sam!' His warning voice cut through her delaying tactics. Heaving a sigh, and displaying reluctance in every sinew of her body, she responded and took the window seat—now occupied by next door's opportunist cat.

'Your parents—'

'Oh, God,' she interrupted, shaking her head. 'You really shouldn't have said what you did to Dad. He can,' she explained with a grimace, 'take things a little literally.'

'What did I say that I should not have?'

'That he can rely on you to do the right thing. Your idea of the right thing and my dad's are not going to be the same,' she explained.

'And what does Dr Maguire mean by *the right thing*?'

'Marriage. I know,' she inserted, before he had an opportunity to laugh or look horrified, 'he does come over as a bit old-fashioned. But I'm his only daughter and—well, I suppose he *is* old-fashioned,' she admitted.

'I do not consider your father old-fashioned.'

She stared at him. 'You don't?'

Alessandro shook his head. 'Your father feels that a man must take responsibility for his own actions. He believes that a child needs and deserves the security of two parents.'

'Well, obviously—in an *ideal* world—'

'The world,' he cut in, his expression severe, 'is what we make of it. We should not use society's imperfections as an excuse to shirk doing the right thing.'

'Perhaps you should marry my father,' she joked with a thin smile. 'You sound like a match made in heaven.'

'I think a successful relationship requires a little friction to keep it lively, and given the circumstances it would be more appropriate for me to marry your father's daughter.'

Sam, her expression wary but still totally confident he had misspoken, corrected him.

'*I'm* my father's daughter.'

His eyes remained trained on her face, his expression aggravatingly enigmatic as he shrugged and said, 'Your point being…?'

'My point being that even as tasteless jokes go, that one is more tasteless than most.'

'You think me proposing is a joke?'

'You're not proposing,' she told him.

A muscle along his jaw clenched, and then clenched again harder as his eyes captured Sam's. 'I would be interested to know what you think I am doing.'

Her mouth opened as she searched his face. 'You want us to get married…sorry, you think we *should* get married.' Clearly *wanting* did not enter into this.

'There is no other option.'

'This is a knee-jerk reaction,' she explained, thinking there could not be a worse time to learn that her lover had a very strongly developed sense of duty. 'Understandably, you're not thinking straight right now. But fortunately for you I am. Tomorrow,' she predicted, 'you're going to realise that you had a narrow escape. Less scrupulous women would have said yes and got it in writing.'

'You are not scrupulous—you are an idiot!'

'I would be if I married you... God, Alessandro, it would be a total disaster. People don't get married because they're pregnant.'

'They do—every day of the week.'

'Well, *I* don't. The only reason I'd get married is if I was in love with a man.' She spread her hands, inviting him to see that she was right.

His expression like granite, he locked his dark eyes onto hers. 'And you don't love me?' His shrug suggested to Sam that he was indifferent to the fact. 'Well, that may be so, but the man you love is not the father of your baby.' A nerve clenched in his lean cheek as he added, 'I am.'

It took several seconds before it clicked and Sam realised he was talking about Jonny. She opened her mouth to put him straight, then almost immediately realised that it might be easier to let him carry on thinking she still carried a torch for the younger man.

'Yes, Alessandro, you're the father. But that doesn't alter the fact that we don't have a blessed thing in common. We weren't even going out; we were staying in. The only thing we had going for us was...' Her eyes slid from his as she swallowed and added hoarsely, 'Sex. And now I'm pregnant we don't even have that!'

A spasm of anxiety crossed his lean features as he rose impetuously to his feet. 'Why? Is there a problem, medically speaking?'

She shook her head. 'No, I'm fine.'

'Your doctor has not advised you not to—?'

'No, nothing like that,' she inserted hastily. 'Actually, I haven't seen the doctor yet. There's not much point—I'm only—'

'*Not seen a doctor…?*'

Reading the shocked outrage in his taut features, Sam groaned. 'There's no point, Alessandro. Not until…'

'I think there is every point.'

'Fine…fine… Have it your way.' On this she was willing to humour him. 'I'll arrange something.'

'I will come with you.'

Sam shook her head. 'That isn't going to happen.'

The flat pronouncement caused his eyes to darken. 'I will not be delegated some peripheral role here…'

'Unless you want to give birth, you've not much option,' she rebutted, with a calm she was far from feeling.

Married to Alessandro… It was so tempting—but she knew that she couldn't agree, no matter how much she wanted to. She hadn't been able to cope with the stresses of a loveless affair. It stood to reason that a loveless marriage would be about a million times worse!

Concealing her true feelings had become next to impossible by the end, and Sam doubted she would be able to keep up the façade for five minutes if they were living together.

Alessandro got to his feet and stalked towards her. Laying his hands on the sill at either side of her, he leaned forward. 'You *will* marry me. My child will not be denied his father.'

She looked into his dark eyes. He was close enough for her to see the faint white line that ran along his temple. An image of him lying on the stretcher, with blood seeping from the gaping wound in his forehead, flashed into her head and she went pale.

His hand came up to cup her face. 'What's wrong?'

'Nothing,' she denied, jerking her chin from his grasp. 'I'm not trying to deny the baby a father. You're the father, and nothing can change that,' she admitted, rubbing a finger across the bridge of her nose and avoiding his eyes. 'But I'm afraid that for once in your life, Alessandro, you have to accept that yours isn't the final word on this. Mine is.'

'That has been the case from the start.'

'What?' she said, utterly astounded at his angry, brooding claim.

'You have laid down the rules and I,' he observed grimly, 'have meekly fallen in line. That is going to stop.'

She stopped rubbing her nose and gaped at him. *Alessandro…? Meek…?*

'Is that a fact?'

'You don't know what you are taking on. Being a single parent is not easy.'

If she could cope with loving a man who didn't love her back, Sam felt she could cope with almost anything. 'And you would know all about that, I suppose?'

'Katerina was eleven when I became her guardian.'

The reminder made Sam flush.

'You know that what I'm saying makes sense,' he added.

Sam shook her head mutely. Sense didn't enter into it. She loved him, and that made no sense, but she could no more change the situation than she could her own fingerprints!

'You *will* marry me,' he said, fastening the buttons on his shirt. 'When you see sense,' he added, 'you know where to find me.' Striding to the door, his back stiff and unyielding, he didn't look back once.

If he had, the tears spilling down her white face might have made him reconsider his exit.

CHAPTER THIRTEEN

THE building had incredible views over the river, a startling glass frontage, and bore no identifying logo.

Sam paid the cab driver and eyed the modern edifice with an uncertain frown. 'This *is* the Di Livio Building…?'

'It is, love,' he promised. 'For my money you can't beat Georgian architecture. But what do I know…? This won all sorts of awards, apparently.'

Sam, her thoughts a long way from the merits of modern architecture, handed the man a tip and straightened her shoulders before approaching the building. She paused, briefly succumbing to panic, before she stepped into the revolving doors. Catching sight of her image in the large glass panels and realising she was dressed for going round the supermarket, she carried on walking and ended up where she'd started—outside looking in.

This has to stop, she told herself. Alessandro isn't going to notice what you're wearing.

Actually, they were the same clothes she'd been wearing when he'd proposed. Not really the sort of outfit a girl should wear when the man in her life asked her to marry him. But then it hadn't been that sort of proposal… To her mind it had been more in the nature of an ultimatum.

But then Alessandro was an ultimatum sort of man.

It had been less than twenty-four hours since Alessandro,

not a man accustomed to hearing no, had stormed off, saying that when she came to her senses she knew where to find him. She had never known a man so prone to slinging around ultimatums… The problem was, Sam reflected dully, he generally didn't have to wait long—at least where she was concerned!

He said, *You will,* she responded with an equally determined, *Never,* and five minutes later she was panting to fall in with his plans. It was not a good precedent to set, but she was very aware after the last twelve hours' events that there were more important things at stake than her pride or proving a point.

It wasn't until she had walked out of the hospital that morning and the taxi driver had asked her where she wanted to go that Sam had found the flaw in Alessandro's parting shot— she *didn't* know where to find him!

She didn't have the faintest idea where he lived, worked, or for that matter if he was still in the country. In the faint hope that her taxi driver would not be as ignorant as she was, she had said, 'The Di Livio offices…' and got a cheery, 'Right you are, love,' in return.

As for coming to her senses—that sort of depended on your definition. As far as Sam was concerned coming to her senses involved waking up one morning and not being in love with her Italian lover.

That hadn't happened. She suspected that it probably never would—not that she'd actually been to bed yet.

The phone had rung a bare two hours after Alessandro had stormed off, and Sam still hadn't cooled down.

It obviously hadn't even crossed his mind that she wouldn't come crawling. Well, if he was waiting for her, he'd wait a damned long time. A person would have to be totally insane to marry such a pompous, opinionated, dyed-in-the wool male chauvinist. Of course he was also the man who could make her skin tingle, who could make her feel sassy, sexy and generally irresistible. Never seeing him again might mean she would never have those feelings again. No *might* about it.

I want to feel that way again!

Pushing aside the intrusive thought, Sam had concentrated on all the things she wouldn't miss about him. For a start he was always prepared to think the worst of her—the cheque situation being a perfect example. And not only was he infuriatingly stubborn, he was congenitally incapable of admitting when he was wrong.

He'd had the cheek to say she had no idea of what she was letting herself in for! She'd taught a class of thirty, for heaven's sake!

Taking a certain grim satisfaction from the fact that she was going to show him—even if it *killed* her—that she was perfectly capable of bringing up their child, she had picked up the receiver still on an angry, defiant high. She would be such a perfect single mother that one day even he would be forced to eat his words. Hopefully he would choke on them.

She had nursed her anger until the moment when she had picked up the phone and heard Rachel's voice.

'Sam—thank God you're there! I d…don't know what to do…'

'Rachel…?' Her friend's voice was hardly recognisable.

It took some time, but Sam eventually got the bones of the story out of her friend. It transpired that Rachel had received a call when she'd got to work that morning from the nanny, who'd said she was concerned about Harry. Rachel had left work immediately, and by the time she'd reached home the nanny had already called for an ambulance. Rachel was ringing Sam from the hospital, where the staff had uttered a word guaranteed to make any parent's blood run cold—*meningitis*.

Sam called a cab and rushed to the hospital. The young nanny who was trying to cope with Rachel greeted her arrival with relief. Rachel greeted her with a tear-stained face and a stream of bitter self-recrimination.

'He's got meningitis, Sam, and it's all my fault! I should have stayed at home. A *good* mother would have stayed at home. What sort of mother puts a meeting before her child? I just thought he had a cold…he did say his head was hurting…'

'Rachel, there's no way you could have known…'

'That's what I've been telling her,' said the young nanny. 'Anybody would have thought he had a cold. *I* thought he had a cold. It wasn't until his mum had gone that he really went off,' she explained to Sam. 'The doctors say that it happens that way sometimes. But they all say we got him here very quickly, and that's good.'

Between them, Sam and the young nanny, who both felt pretty inadequate to the task, tried their best to support the distraught young mother through the evening and interminable night.

This morning the doctors were cautiously optimistic—although they were making no promises.

Sam and the nanny persuaded Rachel, who had barely left her child's side since she'd been allowed in the ITU, to come and get a drink.

Rachel, her face waxen with fear and exhaustion, sat and sipped her tea. 'I wish Simon was here. I don't even know if he got my message. New York…' she said, her voice wobbling. 'So f…far away. I just don't know what to do. Simon would know what to do. You two have been great, of course, but…'

'We're not Simon.' Sam nodded understandingly. 'He'll be here soon, Rachel,' she promised, hoping like hell he wouldn't make her a liar.

It was ten minutes later when Simon, who *had* got the message, walked into the small lounge where the three women were sitting.

Sam just knew that she would never forget the look on Rachel's face when she saw her husband. She had seen another side of being a single parent, and quite frankly she no longer thought she was up to the task.

The disaster that had torn apart Rachel's perfect life last night had had the effect of putting her own concerns in perspective, and now gave Sam the strength to walk boldly into the lobby.

'Hang in there, Rachel,' she murmured, crossing her fingers.

The interior of the cutting-edge building had so many reflective surfaces that Sam blinked, momentarily blinded as she entered under the watchful eyes of two uniformed but discreet security guards. The woman seated in a reception area flanked by two metal sculptures was blonde, and groomed to within an inch of her life. Her nails ruled out a lifestyle that involved strenuous tasks like taking the lid off a jar. Women who looked like her were the reason Sam never shopped for clothes in certain smart designer shops.

Now, however, was not a time to be intimidated by a snooty expression and killer nails. Deciding on the direct approach, Sam marched up and with a confident smile announced, 'I'd like to see Mr Di Livio.' She'd reserve the bolshiness in case the direct approach didn't work.

The pencilled brows of the woman behind the desk rose and she looked faintly amused. 'You have an appointment...?'

Sam felt a flush travel up her neck. 'No, but—'

'I'm afraid that Mr Di Livio doesn't see people without appointments.' She served up another professional smile and a look of pitying condescension before turning her attention to the computer screen in front of her.

About to turn and leave, Sam stopped. *You're acting like a wimp.* Lifting her chin, she said firmly, 'He'll see me.'

The other woman's sleek head lifted. There was a slight hint of exasperation in her professional smile as she addressed Sam. 'There are no exceptions.'

'I'm not going anywhere until I see him.' Even as she made this brave claim, on the periphery of her vision Sam was conscious of a security guard who clearly had other ideas approaching. 'Tell him Sam is here. He'll see me,' she told the other woman. 'Tell him I've changed my mind.'

'Miss, if you'll just…?' The security guard's hand hovered above the sleeve of her denim jacket.

'Tell him I *will* marry him.'

The women's rather protuberant eyes widened to their fullest extent. *'Marry…?'*

Sam was suddenly too mad to be intimidated. 'Be very, *very* sure before you laugh,' she suggested quietly to the other woman, who was tottering on the verge of laughter.

Something in her manner brought a flicker of uncertainty to the other woman's eyes.

'Why don't you just ring upstairs?' Sam suggested.

Before the woman had come to a decision a door behind Sam silently slid open and out stepped Alessandro. He froze mid-stride, his dark brows drawing together as he saw her.

'Sam!'

Deaf to the startled note of pleasure in his deep voice, Sam spun around. The breath left her body as she saw him standing there. Until that point she had not realised how badly she had missed looking at him. *Not even twenty-four hours… Dear God, girl, do you have it bad!*

The pleasure had been replaced by caution as he asked, 'What are you doing here?'

She wanted to say, *I've just realised that I can't bring up our baby on my own. I've realised that if anything bad happens I want you there to hold my hand. And I want you there to share the good things too. The first steps, first words…* Feeling her eyes fill, she blinked and said none of those things—which was just as well, because they would undoubtedly have sent Alessandro running for cover. 'I was passing…'

'I'm assuming that means you have come to your senses?'

She loosed a dry laugh. 'Or lost them,' she retorted.

His feet were silent on the polished Italian limestone floor as he walked towards her. 'I must admit I thought you'd make me wait longer.'

The mocking quality in his voice was something Sam told

herself she had to expect under the circumstances. 'What can I say…?' she asked, lifting her slender shoulders in a shrug. 'I can't imagine my life without you in it?' she suggested, rolling her eyes sarcastically.

When he realised how true this was, as he inevitably would, because Alessandro was far too perceptive not to, she wasn't going to be able to shrug it off. But right now she couldn't think that far ahead.

As he scanned her upturned features the taunting quality left his face. The freckles on her nose stood out starkly against the dramatic pallor of her skin. The purple smudges under her eyes had not been there yesterday.

It was only the presence of others that stopped Alessandro demanding on the spot what she had been doing to herself. The anger that caused his dark eyes to flare was aimed almost entirely at himself. How could he be angry with someone who looked one step away from total collapse. If he'd stuck around, instead of walking out, she wouldn't be in this state… But he hadn't stuck around, and in his eyes the fact that Samantha was stubborn and irrational enough to drive the most tolerant of men crazy was no excuse for his behaviour.

He put his hand under her elbow. 'Cancel my meetings for the rest of the day, Edward,' he said, without taking his eyes from Sam's face.

A younger man, whom Sam hadn't been aware of until that moment, blinked, opened his mouth—presumably to protest—and changed his mind.

'I can come back later if you're busy,' Sam said, thinking, *If you say yes, I'll kill you.*

The fingers around her elbow tightened. 'Actually, you can cancel my meetings until Monday.'

In the car, Alessandro got straight to the point. 'Am I to take it that you will marry me?'

'Am I to take it that you had any doubts?' Without waiting for a response to her quip, she tilted her head to look up at him. 'You do know that it would be easier to get to see the Prime Minister than you?' And definitely easier on her traumatised nervous system, she decided, unable to tear her eyes from his face.

'Why didn't you ring to tell me you were coming?'

Her eyes slid from his. A little creativity, if not outright lying was called for. She could hardly say, *I ripped up your number because I didn't trust myself not to ring you every five seconds.* 'I lost your mobile number. Where are we going?' she added shrilly.

'Somewhere we can talk without interruptions.'

Sam's face scrunched up in dismay. 'God,' she groaned. 'Do we *have* to talk?'

He angled an impatient look at her face. 'We are going to get married. I think you should resign yourself to the inescapable fact that we will of necessity spend some of the next forty years talking.' *But most of it in bed.*

'Forty years!' Sam exclaimed.

'If you want to talk statistics, the average life expectancy of—'

'I don't want to talk…statistics, that is. You're not trying to tell me you expect us to *stay* married, are you?'

'That's what the contract says.'

Sam shot a resentful glance up at his patrician profile. 'We always end up arguing.'

'Only on the occasions we don't end up making love.'

This silky observation reduced her to silence, which lasted until the chauffeur-driven car he had bundled her into drew up outside a row of Georgian terraces. Not that her silence seemed to have bothered Alessandro, who had spent most of the journey hitting keys on a laptop while simultaneously taking calls in several languages. She had heard of multitasking but this was ridiculous… Pressing a hand to her stomach, she wondered if the baby would inherit his IQ.

It was only when she had preceded him up a shallow flight

of stairs that led to an impressive door that Sam realised this wasn't a terrace, but one house. 'You live here?'

'Some of the time.'

'So nursery space is not going to be a problem, then?' she said drily as she entered the marble-floored hallway. 'Good God!'

Alessandro watched, his expression amused, as she did a wide-eyed three-hundred-and-sixty-degree rotation.

'You approve…?'

'I've always wanted to live in a museum—or failing that a really swish mausoleum. You live here *alone*…?' This much space for one man seemed bizarre to someone who had been brought up in an Edwardian semi.

'There are the staff.' As he spoke, one of their number appeared. Alessandro spoke in Italian and the thick-set figure replied in the same language. He nodded in a respectful way towards Sam before vanishing.

'Did you say something to him about me?' she demanded suspiciously.

Alessandro looked amused. 'I said you were thirsty and would like a cup of tea.'

A cup of tea was the very least she needed. 'Who did you say I was? You didn't say anything about us getting married, did you?'

'I am not required to identify my guests, and I do not discuss my private business with my staff. Now, sit down before you fall down and tell me what has happened.'

The addition made Sam blink. Once more his powers of perception were unnerving. 'How do you know something has?'

'It does not take a genius. You are as pale as a ghost and you look as though you haven't been to bed.'

He too had spent a sleepless night. It wasn't every day a man discovered he was about to become a father and had a marriage proposal rejected. For hours he had silently seethed over what he considered her unreasonable behaviour.

'I haven't.' She lifted her hand to her mouth to stifle a yawn. 'I was in hospital all night.'

At her side, Alessandro froze.

'Hospital…?' There was screaming tension in every line of his long, lean body as he scanned her face.

'Yes, I've just come from St Jude's—'

He stared at her, disbelief etched into every line of his taut features. Behind the disbelief lurked fear. 'And you did not contact me?' he cut in, dragging both hands through his hair.

'Contact you? Why should I have?'

'Dio mio, I don't believe you… How can you ask?' He stopped abruptly and, exerting obvious self-control, tempered his tone as he said tersely, 'Sit down.' Sam found herself being urged into a chair. Alessandro squatted down beside her, the strain in his face. 'They let you leave?' His voice suggested he disapproved of the decision. 'You are all right…? The baby…?'

Sam, realising his mistake, shook her head. 'No, it wasn't me—I was there with Rachel. You remember? Harry's mum?' Her voice became suspended by tears as an image of the little boy looking so frail and vulnerable flashed into her head. 'Sorry…'

'Sorry…?'

Her mind still filled with images of the terribly ill toddler who, when she had previously seen him had been so fit and well, she didn't pick up on his tense tone.

'Well, it would have solved your problem, wouldn't it?' It wasn't that she thought he wished their child harm, but any man in his situation would find it tough not to do a bit of *if only*.

Her unthinking reflection caused the remaining colour to leave Alessandro's face. Eyes blazing in a stony set face, he took her by the shoulders.

'You will never ever say such a thing to me again.'

His tone made her flinch. She met his eyes, registered the molten fury in his taut face and realised belatedly how much her throwaway comment had offended him. She knew that it wasn't reasonable to be mad with him for not wanting this baby as much as she did, any more than it was reasonable to be angry with him because he didn't love her back, but Sam couldn't help herself.

She was dismayed to feel her eyes fill up again with weak tears. 'Well, it's true,' she gulped. 'You may not want to hear it, but the fact is it would have made life a lot simpler for you if I *had* been the patient.' She pressed her hands protectively to her belly and swallowed. 'It's not as if you *want* the baby to be here,' she reminded him thickly. 'You'd like it to go away, so that you can get your life back to normal.'

Seeing the single tear rolling down her cheek, he felt some of the icy hauteur fade from his face. 'Have I ever said that?'

Her eyes slid from his. 'You didn't have to. It's obvious,' she countered with a loud, unhappy sniff. 'Any man in your situation would feel that way.'

'I am not any man.'

Sam lifted her eyes to his face and thought, *Tell me something I don't already know!*

A nerve along his strong jaw began to throb. 'Do *you* wish our baby would go away?'

'That's not the same.'

He arched a dark brow. 'You think not?' Sam released a startled gasp as he moved her hands and laid one of his own across her belly. She looked at the big hand, resting warm and firm on her, and her throat closed over with some unidentifiable emotion. 'You are carrying this child, but this baby is half you, half me—a part of both of us. You would lay down your life to save him.'

An overwhelmed Sam blinked up at him and realised that it was a statement, not a question.

'And so,' he added simply, 'would I. Now,' he said, placing a finger under her chin and tilting her face up to his. 'No more crying…'

'Sorry—I don't know what's wrong with me. I suppose,' she said, blowing her nose on the tissue he handed her, 'it's my hormones…. Oh, dear.' She grimaced. 'I swore I wouldn't use that excuse.'

'What happened at the hospital?' He removed his hand from her stomach—a situation Sam viewed with some ambivalence—and sat on the arm of her chair. 'Your friend is ill?'

'No, it's Harry. He's three, Alessandro, just three. It's not fair, is it…?' Sam swallowed, dropped her head, and felt his hand on her hair.

'No, *cara mia*, it is not fair.' As his fingers moved in a strong, sweeping motion down her tense spine she expelled a shuddering sigh and lifted her head.

'He's got meningitis.'

'Dio mio!' Alessandro exclaimed. While of course he felt sympathy for the unfortunate innocent and his parents, his first concern was for Samantha and their unborn child. 'You had contact…?'

She shook her head. 'No, he was in Intensive Care, and they wouldn't let me go in. But I could see him through the glass and he looked so small…and there were tubes…and Rachel kept saying it was her fault…and I couldn't do anything.' Her voice suspended by tears, Sam covered her face with both hands. 'I felt so useless,' she confessed in a muffled voice.

With a muttered imprecation he slid into the chair beside her, pulling her bodily into his arms. Lifting her hair off her neck, he cradled her head in one hand while looking tenderly into her tear-drenched eyes, before pressing her face into his shoulder. 'You were there for your friend when she needed you, Sam. You did what you could.'

Her entire body shook while she wept. Alessandro, judging that the release was what she needed, let her cry herself out.

When the sobs began to subside he stopped stroking her head and urged gently, 'Tell me about it.'

The sobs stopped completely and she lifted her head, turning a tear-stained face to his. 'You don't mean that.'

'I do not say things I do not mean.'

'That makes you a pretty unusual person,' she observed. 'I'm not normally a crying person,' she added with an apologetic grimace. 'Sorry…' she said again, trying to get up from his lap.

His hands tightened around her waist. 'Stay put.'

It was so tempting to obey his casual command. There was something awfully comforting about being in his arms. 'I'm heavy.' She was actually deeply mortified by her emotional outburst, but amazingly he didn't appear half as dismayed as most men she knew would have been in similar circumstances.

He shook his head. 'Heavy! You are like a small bird,' he observed, running a finger along the elegant curve of her collarbone. 'Though mostly you remind me of a sleek, elegant feline. Delicate to look at, but not someone you'd like to face in a fight. You even have the eyes of a Siamese.'

'My being *delicate* doesn't seem to stop you fighting with me,' she muttered.

'With us, fighting is foreplay.' He angled a teasing eyebrow, wicked amusement registering in his dark gaze as she flushed.

'Well, I've not much room for comparison.' When she got up he didn't try and stop her. Sam immediately wished he had.

'I have,' he slotted in, watching her walk towards the baby grand piano that stood in the corner. 'So you must take my word on this. Let me rephrase that. I *suggest* that you take my word on this. I have already learned that issuing a prohibition does not have the desired effect with you. You really are a natural-born rebel.'

This extraordinary analysis of her behaviour made Sam, whose finger was poised above the keys, stare. 'It's not me, it's you. I'd never broken a rule in my life before I met you.'

'Then I must be good for you.' In one flowing motion that

made her stomach flip, he rose and walked to her side. Leaning across her, he pressed a key. 'You play?'

'Not well,' she said, trying hard to disguise what having his brown finger casually skim over her cheek did to her.

'Now, tell me, how is little Harry?'

Sam sighed. 'The doctors weren't giving anything away, but Rachel's nanny was brilliant. She called an ambulance, and apparently in a situation like that minutes can make all the difference. This morning the doctors seemed a little bit more positive, and Simon—Rachel's husband—had arrived, so I was surplus to requirements.'

'You didn't sleep all night?' he observed, scanning her pale upturned features with a frown. 'I know you wanted to offer support to your friend, but in your condition—'

'Rachel doesn't know I'm pregnant,' Sam cut in. 'And I had to go. Simon was in New York, and her parents are in Cornwall. Her dad is pretty frail since his heart attack last year.'

Alessandro pinned the strand of gleaming copper hair that had lain across her cheek behind her ear. 'Her husband arrived this morning…?'

Sam nodded and, unable to resist any longer, rubbed her cheek against his hand, which remained close to her face. 'Apparently,' she said, closing her eyes and smiling weakly, 'he paid a small fortune for a seat on the next flight out. You know, just seeing him this morning seemed to give Rachel strength. It was amazing.'

Alessandro mulled over her words for a moment, then said in a voice that was strangely lacking in emotion, 'So you are marrying me because you think I will make a good father?'

'Well, you will,' she countered, confused by the strong hint of affront in his manner.

'Thank you,' he said, not looking overjoyed by the compliment.

He seemed to be waiting, so she added, 'And a child needs

two parents.' *And I need you.* 'But of course there must be some ground rules.'

Alessandro raised his brows, but didn't interrupt as she continued.

'I'll try not to interfere with your life any more than absolutely necessary…'

His hand fell away from her face. 'That is very good of you,' he said, walking towards the carved Adam fireplace.

'I'm a realist. I just want you to be discreet.'

Alessandro, who had been standing looking at the room reflected in the over-mantel mirror, spun back. 'Can it be that you are giving me permission to take lovers? Does that mean *you* intend to take lovers, to satisfy your newly awakened appetite for sex?'

The colour flew to her face. 'What a question!'

'You introduced the subject,' he pointed out. 'Do you not believe in equality of the sexes?'

'Of course. But I'm surprised if you do.'

'If I am at liberty to seek entertainment outside the marriage bed, would it not be right for you to do the same?'

The thought of any man other than Alessandro touching her filled her with repugnance. 'I'm pregnant,' she reminded him.

'This is not something I am in any danger of forgetting.'

The dry insertion made her eyes slide from his. She didn't need reminding that this marriage wouldn't be happening if it wasn't for the baby.

'When you have my ring on your finger I think you will find that I can satisfy you, and if our relationship continues as it has begun, moral issues aside— Oh, yes,' he said, seeing her expression, 'I *am* acquainted with morals.'

Sam belatedly realised that he was furious. 'I didn't mean that—'

'Moral issues aside,' he gritted, ignoring her, 'I will not have the energy to seek excitement outside the marriage bed.'

'So long as I amuse you.'

Alessandro's accent was significantly stronger as he ground out, 'You do not *amuse* me. You infuriate and provoke me.'

'The feeling's mutual,' she flared.

Alessandro, his jaw clenched, said something under his breath.

Sam's eyes narrowed. 'I'm going to learn Italian, and then you won't be able to do that,' she warned him.

'You want to know what I said? No problem. I said I'm not going to fight with you.'

'Why not?'

'Because we will end up in bed.'

Sam didn't know which upset her more—the assumption that they'd end up in bed, or the implication that it was somewhere he wanted to avoid!

'And, as much as I would like to…you need to rest.'

'I suppose I *should* go home,' she admitted, slightly mollified by his qualification and the frustrated gleam in his eyes.

'No need. You can stay here, where I can keep an eye on you.'

It turned out he meant it quite literally. When Sam woke it was around three in the morning, in a strange bed. It took her a little while to recollect why she was in a strange bed wearing her underwear, and a few seconds longer to notice the figure in the armchair.

Alessandro was sitting with his hands resting on his thighs, his body hunched forward.

'What are you doing?' she asked, struggling into a sitting position.

'Watching you. I like watching you.'

The throaty confidence sent a sharp thrill of sexual excitement through her body. No longer feeling at all sleepy, she threw back the covers and patted the bed. 'You can watch me just as well from here.'

Even though he was sitting several feet away, she could hear the raw sound of his harsh inhalation.

'I like to watch you too,' she said as he rose to his feet, a dark, shadowy figure. 'Even if you just want to sleep,' she added, in case he thought she was being pushy.

Sam heard the sound of a zip being unfastened and swallowed.

'You will find, *cara*, that I actually need very little sleep.' But one thing Alessandro had discovered he could not do without was a redhead with eyes like the sea…

CHAPTER FOURTEEN

THE wedding took place a week later, in a tiny chapel on Alessandro's Tuscan estate which was just as spectacularly lovely as Emma had suggested.

There were few people in attendance. Besides her parents, Sam had invited Emma and Paul. Other than his sister and Dorothy Smith, Alessandro had invited half a dozen close friends, but the only one Sam was conscious of was the dark-haired beauty who appeared to be in tears when she embraced Alessandro after the ceremony. Marisa Sinclair.

Sam sealed her feelings behind a frozen smile, while inside her hurt and fury silently grew. Neither emotion found any release until after the wedding meal, which had been served in a room where the ceiling was covered in the most incredible frescoes. They and their guests, carrying drinks, had drifted out through the wide doors into the *palazzo* gardens.

Sam was talking to the best man, whom she would have considered the best-looking male she had even seen if she hadn't seen Alessandro first, when Emma hurried over. She thrust a slim mobile phone at Sam and announced, 'You'll want to hear this personally.'

As Sam stood there, emotional tears of relief streaming down her cheeks, Emma explained to the best man, 'Our friend's little boy has been very ill in hospital, and the doctors have just given him the all-clear.'

When Sam had finished talking to Rachel, Emma took back the phone.

'Kind of makes the day perfect, don't you think?' she said happily. 'Will you tell Alessandro the good news or shall I…?'

'You do it,' said Sam.

'Any idea where…?' began Emma, looking around.

Look for the gorgeous brunette and you should find him, thought Sam, but said, 'I think he was on the terrace.'

Sam had just finished receiving a lecture on the antiquity and history of the *palazzo* from Dorothy Smith when Alessandro materialised at her side.

'Do you mind if I borrow my bride for one minute, Smithie?'

'Well, considering you have her for the rest of your life I consider that selfish. But who am I to stand in the way of true love?'

Sam was so embarrassed by the comment that she couldn't even look at Alessandro as he drew her indoors.

'A lot of books,' she said, looking around the room—anywhere rather than at him as he closed the door. In her head she was seeing the beautiful lawyer with her arms wound around his neck. She pressed her fingers to her drumming temples. Suddenly crimes of passion made a lot more sense.

'That is not uncommon for a library.'

Sam made herself look at him. He looked, of course, totally incredible. Every long, lean inch of him so rampantly male that her stomach muscles quivered. 'What do you want, Alessandro?' she asked, wiping her damp palms along the silk skirt of her wedding gown.

'I want a wife who can behave with some degree of circumspection,' he announced frigidly.

Sam did not have to pretend total incomprehension as she stared at him. 'What…?' For the first time she registered the anger in his body language.

'You will *not* make assignations with Jonny Trelevan.'

Sam's wide eyes attached themselves to the nerve leaping in his lean cheek.

'In fact,' he decreed autocratically, 'as you obviously have no self-control or sense of what is fitting where he is concerned, in the future you will not be alone with that man.'

The throbbing silence stretched, until Sam drew a long, shaky breath and, planting her hands on her slim hips, walked towards him. 'For starters,' she said, her voice shaking as she fought to control her anger, 'I haven't the faintest idea what you are talking about…*assignations…*?'

Alessandro's lip curled contemptuously as he dragged a hand through his dark hair. 'Before we dined you vanished, and so did Trelevan.' One dark brow elevated. 'A coincidence?' he suggested. 'I don't think so.'

'You think I—?' She broke off, shaking her head incredulously as she drew in air through her flared nostrils. 'I'm really touched by your faith in me,' she choked bitterly, 'and I'm sorry I can't live down to your expectations of me. But if you had taken the trouble you might also have noticed that my mother was not in the room either. I spilled some wine on my dress.' She touched her shaking hand to the spot on the pearl-encrusted bodice of her gown where the liquid had spilled. 'Mum was sponging it off. You could always ask her to confirm my story—though of course,' she added sarcastically, 'she might be covering for me…'

The muscles in Alessandro's brown throat worked as his eyes locked with hers. 'Your *mother…*?'

Sam nodded, and watched the dark colour rise up his neck.

His jaw tightened another notch, and a hint of defensiveness entered his voice as he said, 'Trelevan was not in the room.'

'You really do have a nerve, Alessandro.'

'I might,' he conceded stiffly, 'have made a mistake.'

'I *know* I've made a mistake. I walked up the aisle,' she retorted, too angry to notice that her comment had made the colour leave his face. 'You're acting like a little boy who doesn't want to share his toys with another kid.' As she saw the incredulous anger flare in his eyes she realised the analogy might have been better.

'*Madre di Dio,* I am a *man* who doesn't want to share his *wife* with another *man*. And if you flout me on this, Samantha, you will find I do more than throw a tantrum.'

'I don't think under the circumstances anyone would blame me for slipping off into the shrubbery for a snog.' Ignoring his hissing inhalation, Sam continued in the same hard, angry voice. 'My h…husband invites his mistress to the wedding!' she yelled. 'And then has the cheek to fling around ultimatums!'

'I have no idea what you're talking about.' Alessandro, conscious of the dull roar of blood thundering in his ears, could see very little but the image her angry words had implanted in his skull. His wife in another man's arms.

Sam released an incredulous laugh. 'I'm talking,' she told him, 'about Marisa Sinclair—your mistress—who you expect me to smile at and say *Delighted to meet you.* Well, I'm *not*!' she cried, catching her trembling lower lip between her teeth and dashing the tears from her eyes with the back of her hand. 'I'm not at all happy!'

A shuttered look came over his face. 'Marisa is an old and valued friend.'

'Oh, is that what they call it now?' she sneered. 'You know, she is much prettier in the flesh than she looked in the newspapers—but then you already know that, don't you?'

Alessandro studied her face for a moment, before saying quietly, 'You have nothing to fear from Marisa.'

'You mean you're not sleeping with her any longer? Gosh,' she intoned sarcastically, 'I feel better already—because you always tell me the truth.'

'I do not wish to discuss my relationship with Marisa with you. It is not relevant to us.' Alessandro, whose breathing had steadied, added softly, 'You've never seemed jealous that Jonny has Katerina, but the idea of me with Marisa…'

'I'm not in—' Sam stopped abruptly, her eyes sliding from his as the colour rushed to her pale cheeks. 'I'm not married to him. Now,' she went on backing towards the door, 'I need to get out of this—' she fingered the strapless neckline of her wedding gown '—if we're to get back to London tonight.'

'Did I say? You look very beautiful today, Samantha.'

His accented voice sent shivers up her spine.

'No, you didn't say,' she admitted huskily as, her hand on the door handle, she spun back. She glanced down at the slim silk dress that revealed the creamy upper slopes of her breasts and clung to her still-slender waist before flaring out from the hip to swish sexily around her legs. 'My mum helped me choose it.'

'The dress?' He dismissed the designer creation with a graceful wave of his hand. 'I was not talking about the dress. I am sorry we have to get back tonight, but I promise we *will* have a honeymoon.'

She was within a hair's breadth of responding to the earthy invitation in his eyes when she recalled that he had offered no concrete explanation or even an apology for Marisa Sinclair's presence. Lips set in a hard line, she enquired bitterly, 'Is Marisa coming too?'

As she fled, before he could respond to her sarcastic retort, it hit her: *I'm married.* No matter how many times she said it, it still didn't feel real.

The next day, back in London, her sense of unreality persisted. They had arrived so late the night before that she had fallen asleep fully dressed on the big four-poster. When she'd woken later that night she'd been wearing her underclothes. In the darkness she had made out Alessandro's profile. She'd lain there listening to the even sound of his breathing, experiencing a longing as strong as the one which caused her to breathe—a longing to feel his skin against her own, to taste him, to merge with him.

It had been only the memory of their unresolved argument and the painfully awkward journey back to London that had held her back.

It was light when she next woke, and Alessandro was already up and dressed. She barely had time to register his silent presence at her bedside and recall that he was now her husband, even if she didn't feel married, when she had to dash to the bathroom.

Her morning sickness was particularly vile, and she was soon on her knees in the bathroom—a great image of his wife for him to carry through the day when he had to leave!

When a guilty-sounding Emma rang before lunch, Sam was glad of the interruption.

'I know this is the cheekiest thing to ask you when you're on your honeymoon—'

'A honeymoon requires two people,' Sam inserted drily. 'Ask away. The truth is, I'd be glad of the distraction.'

'You know I've got that interview this afternoon—which is why we flew back this morning?'

'Problem with the interview?'

'Not the interview—my sitter. Paul was going to watch Laurie, but his boss has just rung and there's some enormous crisis. So…?'

'Bring her on over,' said Sam.

'You look…' Emma's glance dropped down Sam's slim body. 'Actually, you look terrible,' she observed with a frown.

As if she needed any reminder that she look drained and terrible. 'Sorry I can't live up to *your* high standards, superwoman.'

'I was just saying…and I'm *not* superwoman,' Emma protested.

Sam rolled her eyes. 'What would you call someone who goes into labour on a building site and drives herself to the hospital *after* sorting out a building regulations wrangle? You,' Sam contended, only half joking, 'are one of those women who make the rest of us feel inadequate.' Or me, at least. With her constant tiredness and mood swings, not to mention the nausea, Sam was quite aware that she did not resemble the glowing image of motherhood so often portrayed on the covers of magazines.

'I had morning sickness,' Emma protested.

'No, you had heartburn. Once. After eating a hot curry.' Sam, who was unclipping the harness that secured Laurie in her buggy, stopped what she was doing and angled a questioning look at her best friend. 'Why are you whispering?'

Emma raised her brows and looked around the painting-lined walls of the formal drawing room. 'I feel like I'm being watched,' she admitted. 'Not exactly cosy, is it? Oh, my, that's a real Monet, isn't it? And is that a—?'

'They're all real,' Sam admitted guiltily as she bent down to extract her goddaughter from her buggy.

Emma began to study the carpet she was standing on. 'I'm assuming this is priceless or something?' she said rubbing her toe cautiously into the soft pile of the Aubusson rug. 'You know, on second thoughts, I think it might be better to leave Laurie in the buggy—safer…'

'Don't you dare!' Sam retorted. 'A few grubby fingerprints will make the place more homely.'

An hour later, with toys strewn all over the floor and the remnants of the sandwich lunch they had chosen to eat cross-legged on the floor, it was even homier.

'I hope that's non-toxic,' Sam said to herself as she removed a crayon from Laurie's mouth.

Laurie released a childish cry of anger.

'I prefer the orange myself,' Sam said, and remembered the DVD that Emma had said soothed the baby. Putting down the fractious tot, she inserted it in the machine. Muttering under her breath, she tried to turn it on, but when she pressed the appropriate buttons all she got was a montage of television channels. She tried again, and got the channels again—but this time minus the sound.

She glared at the offending remote. 'Damn! Where is—?' She lifted her head from the remote to look at the screen and stopped dead, the colour fading dramatically from her face as the remote slipped from her fingers and onto the floor. The baby in her arms, she sank down until she was sitting cross-legged on the floor, staring at the screen.

The subtitles beneath the picture for the benefit of the hard of hearing—or people unable to locate the volume on the remote—pronounced that amongst the famous people present for a charity luncheon was Mr Alessandro Di Livio, a generous benefactor.

Alessandro's lean, photogenic face filled the screen—until the woman sitting beside him leaned across, blocking him from the camera's view. Sam went cold inside as the woman tilted her head and laughed up at her handsome companion.

It was Marisa Sinclair.

You could see why so many people had predicted that the clever lawyer would end up marrying Alessandro. She did look the part. Elegant and beautifully groomed, she was wearing a slim-fitting cream silk jacket, cut low to display her cleavage and lots of smooth, tanned flesh.

'Not a freckle in sight!' To cut off her hysterical-sounding laugh Sam pressed a hand to her mouth and turned away from the screen.

No wonder Alessandro hadn't laughed at her crack about the other woman coming along on the honeymoon! Some 'negotiations' he'd had to rush back for.

It was one thing to have a mistress. It was another entirely to flaunt the fact. Actually, no, she thought, brushing a tear angrily from her cheek. The having was just as unacceptable as the flaunting.

They had married in order to give their child a stable environment. And even if *she* hadn't see this televisual proof personally there were plenty of people who knew them both who would have. Clearly he didn't care if the rest of the world knew their marriage was a sham, and clearly he cared even less about humiliating *her*!

Or maybe he hadn't thought? Maybe he couldn't help himself around Marisa Sinclair? A victim to blind lust or love… Either option made Sam equally furious.

Breathing hard, her paper-white face set in hard, angry lines, she forced herself to look at the screen. The camera remained on Marisa Sinclair. Her lovely lips were moving. Sam had no doubt that her words were as sincere as the expression on her lovely face. The strength of the hatred she felt for the other woman was shocking.

If she had stopped long enough to think about the consequences she might not have done it… But what had Alessandro said? *Any woman worth her salt would fight for the man she loved.* Well, she was going to fight. Of course it might have been easier minus the fretful child in her arms…

Entry to the charity event proved a lot easier than she had expected. The name Di Livio certainly opened doors—either that, or people were scared of saying no to a dangerous-looking madwoman carrying a screaming baby.

Muttering about the shallowness of people who were willing to overlook anything if you were rich enough or famous enough, her head held high, she stalked down the carpeted hallway.

As she stepped through the open double doors that led to the flower bedecked ballroom the adrenaline high that had got her this far took a sudden dip. *Bad timing*, she thought, looking around a room filled with smartly dressed and in many cases famous people. A plus point was that so far nobody had noticed her—they were all too busy enthusiastically clapping the minor royal who was at that moment stepping down from the dais set up at one end of the room.

Sam took a moment to stiffen her resolve. As she scanned the room her narrowed gaze skipped over the well-known faces she saw. There was only one face she was interested in, and when she saw it the breath caught in her throat.

Closing her eyes momentarily, she sucked in a big breath and straightened her shoulders. *Any woman worth anything would fight for the man she loved.* As she wove her way through the tightly packed tables she gathered more and more attention. But Sam was past caring.

It wasn't Alessandro but Marisa who noticed her.

Sam watched as, in response to the scarlet fingers tugging at his sleeve, Alessandro bent his head towards his companion. At her urgent murmur he lifted his head. Sam was close enough to see the shock in his eyes when he saw her.

You can run, buster, but you can't hide, she thought viciously.

Actually, Alessandro showed no inclination to run or hide. He rose in an almost languid manner to his feet and waited, one eyebrow raised, for her to reach his table. By the time Sam reached her goal her breath was coming in short, breathy gasps, and she had the attention of just about every eye in the room.

'Who is that child?' Alessandro asked, as though the baby in her arms was the most unusual aspect of his wife appearing unannounced at this glittering public event, wearing jeans and a T-shirt with orange crayon down the front, while he was playing footsie with his girlfriend.

'It's Laurie. I'm babysitting for Emma,' she snarled.

His dark eyes moved over the baby. 'She has grown.'

'That's what babies do…at least the females do. Emotionally, most males never make it past puberty.' Sam shot her husband a look of pure loathing. 'Sorry to crash your cosy assignation, Marisa…' she gritted, all the time glaring at Alessandro.

'I would not choose to hold an assignation, cosy or otherwise, in the full view of television cameras. Why are you here, Sam?'

'I came—' Sam stopped. What was she supposed to say? *I came here to tell your girlfriend to back off, to tell her that you're mine...*

As a wave of desolation washed over her, her shoulders slumped, and she turned her head momentarily into the soft sweet-smelling curls of the baby in her arms. Even the baby smell could offer her no comfort.

'It doesn't matter.'

'Well, now you are here, you will sit down and have a drink with us.'

Sam stared at him. 'I will what?'

'And smile—people are looking.'

'Is that all you care about? What people will think?' The inner rage she felt suddenly exploded inside her head like crystal shattering. 'Well, let's see what they think of this, shall we?'

Sam managed to pick up a glass and throw its contents in Alessandro's face in one smooth motion.

She knew that the image of his incredulous rage as he stood there with wine dripping down his face would be etched permanently in her brain. And she knew with equal certainty that Alessandro would never forgive her for humiliating him in public this way.

'It could have been worse. It could have been red.'

She managed not to start crying until she was safely back in the taxi.

CHAPTER FIFTEEN

MARISA SINCLAIR, whose dark, glossy head had been tilted back whilst she admired the chandeliers overhead, turned as she heard the echo of Sam's shoes on the marble floor of the hall.

'I've always loved this place.'

And you'd look so at home here, Sam thought, imagining the brunette gracefully ascending the sweeping staircase, diamonds glittering at her lovely throat. The image increased the tight feeling in her chest.

'I prefer something a little cosier.' *Me, I'd spoil my big entrance by falling flat on my face.* 'If you came expecting me to apologise, forget it. I'm not sorry. Alessandro isn't here—but I expect you already know that.'

Encountering the frigid touch of Sam's eyes, the older woman winced. 'You really don't like me, do you? And I don't actually blame you,' she admitted.

'That's *terribly* good of you.'

The butler, who had notified Sam of her visitor's arrival, responded to Sam's nod and retreated, leaving the two women alone.

'He's protective…' Marisa observed, as the austere-looking thickset Italian vanished from view. 'I virtually had to refuse to budge before he agreed to tell you I was here.'

Sam's brows lifted as she flashed the other woman a cold smile. 'And why *are* you here?'

'I came because I think there are some things you should know.'

Presumably that my husband loves you? She looked at the woman with a frozen expression. 'And you decided that someone should be you?'

'Well, I know Alessandro isn't going to tell you.'

'Decided to spare my feelings has he? Well, I think it's a bit late for that, don't you?'

Marisa's feathery brows twitched into a frown. 'Alessandro *couldn't* tell you. He's the sort of man who doesn't break promises.'

This admiring comment drew an ironic laugh from Sam's pale lips.

The concern in the older woman's dark eyes deepened as she scanned Sam's pale features. 'You look terrible.'

Of course I look terrible. My husband skipped his honeymoon so he could spend the day with you. Does she think I've not got the message? The idea that this woman had come to drive the message home sent a shaft of revitalising anger through Sam.

'Did Alessandro send you?' she demanded.

'Good God, no. He doesn't know I'm here!' Marisa exclaimed. The guilty little glance over her shoulder that she could not repress seemed to suggest that she was telling the truth. 'When he finds out,' she admitted cheerfully, 'he'll probably kill me.'

'Your secret is safe with me.'

The older woman responded to Sam's promise with an unexpected high-pitched laugh that made Sam realise for the first time that for once the other woman was neither serene or calm. 'Secrets,' she said, heaving a sigh. 'Secrets are the problem.'

Mystified by this cryptic utterance, Sam shrugged. 'If you say so. Myself, I thought it was more to do with cheating husbands.'

Marisa shook her head hard enough to dislodge a few

strands of glossy dark hair from the chignon she wore. 'Alessandro has not been unfaithful to you…at least not with me. The only thing Alessandro has been to me and Timothy is a good friend, and I'm afraid,' she admitted with a shame-faced grimace, 'we have abused that friendship.'

'Sleeping with his oldest friend's wife hardly makes Alessandro the innocent party.'

'But—'

Cutting across the other woman's protest, Sam said wearily, 'You'd better come in,' and opened the door that led to the morning room.

Sam stood with her shoulders braced against the wall, breathing in the heady scent of the winter jasmine she had cut the previous day. She knew the fragrance would forever be associated in her mind with this day, when Alessandro's mistress had come to stake her claim. The day she realised that she had lost her husband before she had even won him.

'Good thriller,' Marisa observed, picking up the paperback Sam had been reading from the table.

Sam's brows lifted. 'Books…husbands… Who knows what else we have in common?'

Marisa didn't respond to Sam's acid jibe, but continued to pace around the sun-filled room.

'I hate to hurry you, but I have other things to do.' Such as what? she asked herself. Find a good divorce lawyer? The reality of what was happening suddenly hit her with the force of a tidal wave. Her anger and aggression evaporated…and it turned out they were the only things keeping her standing.

'I—' Turning, Marisa saw Sam sway, and with a cry of alarm ran to her side. 'That's it—sit down there,' she said, dragging Sam a couple of steps towards the nearest chair. As Sam sank into it she gave a heavy sigh of relief. 'Can I get you something? Water…?' She looked around the room as if seeking inspiration. 'I'm totally hopeless when people are ill,' she confessed in a tone of self-disgust. 'Shall I ring for some tea?'

Conscious that if she tried to speak the sobs that were aching for release in her throat would escape, Sam shook her head mutely.

'Well, you just sit there…' Marisa recommended.

Sam, who couldn't have done anything else even had she felt the urge to do so, almost smiled.

'Yes, you sit—and I'll talk…' she said. 'Tim and I knew each other when we were growing up, and I always thought I would marry him… I suppose that seems pretty strange to you?'

Sam touched her tongue to the salty beads of moisture that dotted her upper lip. The faintness had passed, but she still felt nauseous. 'As a matter of fact, no, it doesn't.' Though the fact that she had ever mistaken her feelings for Jonny for love now seemed almost laughable.

'Have you ever wanted something so much that you'd do anything to get it, but when you do it's not at all what you expected? Well, that was what being married to Tim was like for me…anticlimax I suppose would be the best word. It wasn't a bad marriage, we were friends, but there were no…fireworks. If you take my meaning.'

'So you looked elsewhere for fireworks?' *And found them!*

Marisa shook her head. 'No, not me. Tim. He came to me and told me he'd met someone. He said he'd fallen in love with his secretary.'

'Not very original.'

Marisa gave a mirthless laugh. 'You think…? Tim's secretary was not only tall, blond, beautiful and a *cordon bleu* cook, but I think the fact he shared Tim's passion for Man United was actually the all-important factor that swung it. How,' she asked with an ironic shrug, 'could I compete with that?'

'He…?'

Marisa laughed at her expression and sank down gracefully in a chair opposite. 'Yeah—he. It seems Tim had been in denial about his sexuality for years. When I said I wanted a divorce he panicked. He said if people found out that he was gay his political career would be over.'

'There are gay politicians,' Sam protested weakly. *Could this be true?*

'True, but none that get voted in on the clean-living, family values ticket. And even if that wasn't the case Tim didn't want to come out. That was where Alessandro came in. He walked into the middle of a big row we were having one day. Considering how *not* shocked he was when Tim told him he was gay,' she recalled thoughtfully, 'I think he'd already suspected. But then I expect you've noticed it's really hard to pull the wool over Alessandro's eyes.'

Sam's gave a gasp, her eyes widening. 'My God—you asked him to pretend to be your lover!' *Or was it pretend…?*

'No, that was his idea.' She angled a shrewd look at Sam's face. 'I wouldn't have minded things getting real,' she admitted. 'But he wasn't interested.'

The relief that had flooded through Sam when she realised that Alessandro wasn't in love with this woman suddenly turned to horror. 'Oh, no!' she gasped. 'What have I done?'

The older woman gave a grimace of sympathy and patted her shoulder.

After Marisa had left, Sam wandered out to the walled rear garden. It began to rain, which suited her mood. She tried to sort out her thoughts, but realised almost immediately that there wasn't much to sort. It was all pretty straightforward.

She had in a matter of minutes effectively killed stone-dead any chance she'd had of any sort of relationship with Alessandro.

She ran her finger over the wet face of a stone heron and sighed. 'He's just never going to forgive me for this,' she said, seeing his face again as the wine had hit him.

'Who is not going to forgive you?'

The colour drained from her face as she spun around to see her husband, standing there watching her.

'What are you doing here?' Her eyes were drawn to the stains down the front of his once white shirt.

'I would have been here sooner had another hysterical woman not waylaid me. Though this one did not throw wine in my face.'

'Hysterical woman...?'

'Katerina. I was just about to get in my car when she arrived. It took me the best part of an hour to get her to calm down enough to tell me what was wrong. When she did, I drove her home.'

'What was wrong?'

'She's pregnant.'

'Pregnant!'

'And it would seem that she's afraid to tell her husband.'

'What?' ejaculated Sam. 'Jonny hasn't told her! He's such an *idiot*!'

As this heartfelt comment was music to Alessandro's ears, he felt he could be generous. 'Having displayed no small degree of idiocy myself recently, I do not feel in a position to throw stones. However, you will be pleased to hear that he has now told her of his money problems—and of your role in helping him out of them.'

Sam struggled to take on board this glut of information. 'What's going to happen?'

'My sister has announced her intention of taking over the running of the stores. Jonny is apparently happy to diversify and use his contacts. Katerina has told him he will leave the finances to her, and utilise his talents crafting individually designed surfboards. Excuse my ignorance, the technicalities passed over my head, but apparently people are prepared to pay a great deal of money for such things...'

'Then they're all right...?'

'I think you could say that my first and only foray into marriage guidance has been a success,' he agreed. 'Would that gaining access to my own home had gone as smoothly…'

'Did you forget your key?' Sam studied his face, which was wet and getting wetter with each passing second. He *had* to be totally furious—but oddly it wasn't fury that was coming across in his facial expression or his body language. But that fury was as far as she got when it came to interpreting the rigidity in his manner.

'No, but when I opened the door Carlo looked as though he would have liked very much to close it in my face…'

Sam gave a confused blink. '*Carlo?* Why would he want to do that?' she asked, genuinely mystified.

One side of Alessandro's mobile mouth lifted. 'It would appear he feels protective towards you, *cara*…'

'*Me?*'

'And not just him. The members of staff who I have encountered so far have all looked at me as though I am some unpleasant sub-species. Still,' he mused, reaching across and taking her chin in his hand, 'I suppose I must get used to being treated like the villain in a Victorian melodrama.'

Sam, whose barely functioning brain had gone into shock when his thumb had slid down the curve of her cheek, was only capable of echoing faintly. 'Victorian melodrama…?' *Why isn't he shouting? Why isn't he yelling? Why isn't he telling me that marrying me is the worst thing he has ever done?*

'Yes. I think it was the crying baby clutched to your breast that captured the imagination of the nation.' He looked around. 'No baby?'

'Paul picked her up.'

Sam looked at him blankly as he cupped the back of her head in his hand and said, 'You're getting very wet,' as he sank his long fingers into her wet hair.

'I don't understand,' she said, grabbing a handful of his shirt to steady herself as her knees started to fold. She was shaking from head to toe.

'There were television cameras there…' he reminded her gently.

'Oh, my God…' As she half closed her eyes she wondered why this should come as such a shock—after all, it had been the television coverage that had prompted her mad *get your hands off my man* crusade.

Unable to contemplate the sheer awfulness of having the most humiliating moment of her life being recorded for posterity, Sam let her head fall forward against his chest. She could feel the warmth of his skin through the dampness of his shirt. She just wanted to close her eyes and lean into his warmth, have his arms close around her and stay that way for ever.

It was several seconds before she could force herself to step back. She swallowed and whispered hoarsely, 'They won't actually show it?'

'From the way my loyal staff have been looking at me, I'd say they already have.'

She gave a groan, amber flecks swirling in her green-blue eyes as they flew, wide and stricken, to his face. 'Couldn't you sue them or something…?'

The total lack of concern he was showing at having his reputation torn to shreds on national television was extremely disconcerting.

His lips curved into a sardonic smile. 'For telling the truth…?'

'The people who write stuff about you wouldn't know the truth if they fell over it!' she exclaimed, unable to hide her indignation at what he had suffered at the hands of the press.

In the act of dragging a hand through his hair, Alessandro stopped. Eye contact was hard to maintain, but he levelled his interrogative stare directly at her wary face. After a moment his hand fell away and comprehension filtered into his dark gaze. 'So Marisa has been talking…?'

Her lips tightened. 'Well, you weren't going to, were you?'

'That was not possible.'

'Oh, I know you'd given your word and all that stuff. And I'm sure it's great having honour and so forth. But forgive me for not patting you on the back. I was the one left thinking…' She caught the strange way he was looking at her and stopped, began to study her hands.

'What were you thinking?'

Her head jerked up. 'Well, what would *you* think if you turned on the TV and saw me next to some gorgeous bloke I had a well-documented history with? Then saw him gaze at me as though looking at me made him hear heavenly music? I know this requires some imagination…'

This bitter addition caused Alessandro, whose expression had been growing increasingly austere as she described this imaginary scenario, to smile. 'Leaving aside the fact that before you entered the room Margaret Danes was the most beautiful woman in the room—'

Sam's eyes widened in protest as she recognised the name of a revered actress who had recently been made a dame. 'Margaret Danes is seventy!' she protested.

'She was a beautiful woman at twenty and she is today. True beauty is not dimmed by the ravages of time. It has to do with an inner glow.'

Midway through his dissertation on beauty, Sam stopped listening. 'Until *I* walked into the room…?' She thought of the way she had marched in, screaming baby under one arm, maniacal gleam in her eyes, and started shaking her head. She didn't stop until he took hold of her chin between his finger and thumb and tilted her face up to him.

'You are a beautiful woman.'

She opened her mouth, but before she could deny this claim she connected with his deep, fabulously dark eyes and lost the power of speech totally. She thought about the incredibly glamorous females who had been present at the glitzy event and looked down at her own jeans. She released a choked laugh. *He had to be joking!*

'And you are my wife,' he finished simply.

The breath snagged in Sam's throat as she lifted her head. Her head started to spin as she registered the incredible tenderness in his face.

'But, leaving aside those factors, you have no history with any man but me. And since you wear my ring on your finger...' Sam trembled a little, but didn't resist as he took her small hand in his. As he stroked his finger against first the plain gold band and then the square-cut emerald in its antique setting she held her breath and tensed expectantly.

The silence stretched, tearing her shredded nerves to breaking point and beyond. The tension was almost unendurable as she waited for him to continue. When he did she jumped and gave a tiny startled cry.

'You never will have history with any other man but me.'

His eyes lifted and melded to hers, and the possessive glow in them sent a corresponding surge of heat through her own body. He released her hand and ran a finger along the soft curve of her cheek until it rested on the small indentation in her chin.

'Don't worry—your future is taken care of, *cara*. I can tolerate a man hearing heavenly music when he looks at you, but if he showed any inclination to do more than gaze at you I would...' His slight smile widened into a wolfish grin. 'Discourage him,' he finished silkily.

'You would?'

He nodded.

Sam, who had started to dare to think that maybe this situation could be saved, took a deep breath and slanted a wary look at him through her lashes. 'I don't blame you for being as mad as hell with me.' *Except he wasn't.* 'If you'd told me this morning that you were going to that darned thing...'

'I was about to tell you this morning, when you announced that you didn't feel married,' he recalled bitterly.

'Did I *say* that?' she gasped.

He nodded. 'It is not what a man enjoys to hear when he

is leaving his wife for the day. Then you had to throw up…that tends to cut short a conversation.'

'I can see that,' she admitted with a rueful grimace. 'I suppose you expect me to explain why I…?'

'Made a national laughing-stock of me?' he inserted. 'No, I don't expect that.'

Her eyes flew to his. They were a deep green. 'You don't?'

He shook his head. 'I already know why you did it.'

She stared up at him.

'You came to fight for your man.' He took her face between both his hands. 'You love me.'

Sam's heart stopped. She opened her mouth and tried to laugh, but nothing but a strangled squeak emerged. The rampant hunger in his eyes made her head spin. 'Marisa is actually very nice,' she heard herself say stupidly. 'We should invite her to dinner some time.'

'Why are we talking about Marisa?' he growled.

'Well, she would have made you a perfect wife.'

'Marisa is beautiful and talented. She probably is perfect,' he admitted. 'But for one thing…'

'What thing?'

A slow smile that made Sam's heart thud spread across his face. 'She isn't you, *tesoro mio*,' he said simply. 'She isn't you, and I have discovered,' he explained against her trembling lips, 'that nothing else will do for me. Say it!'

'Say what?'

'Tell me I'm right—tell me you stormed the ceremony because you were willing to fight for me.' His voice dropped a husky octave as he went on in the same driven tone, 'Tell me that you love me and can't bear the idea of living without me. Tell me that your life without me is empty.'

'All those things,' she gulped.

She felt the deep sigh that shuddered through his lean body. And then, as he angled her face up to his, she recognised the gleam of male triumph in his spectacular eyes. Her eyes closed as he gathered her to him and kissed her—tenderly at first, and then with a growing hunger and lack of control. When he dragged his mouth from hers with a groan he was breathing hard.

'You want me, Alessandro?' she said, wary still of the happiness that was flooding her body.

'I think I loved you from the first moment I saw you.'

'First moment!' she exclaimed, recalling the way he had looked at her on every occasion they had met. 'I don't think so.'

'It's true. I couldn't take my eyes off you. The way you moved, your face, your laugh...' His eyes left hers for a second as he swallowed. 'And then...' His eyes darkened as they met hers. 'Then, Samantha, I saw you look at Trelevan. And I knew that you loved him. I told myself that it was my duty to watch you, to make sure you did not do anything to hurt Katerina.' His lips sketched a derisive smile. 'I carried on telling myself that when I rearranged my schedule time and time again, in order to accept every invitation that came my way if I knew there was a chance you would be there. I couldn't admit that I just wanted to see your face. And the more often I saw it,' he admitted, framing her face in his hands, 'the more I needed to.

'It wasn't until I got you into my bed that I recognised my self-deception for what it was. And then to realise that you had not given yourself to another man... It made me feel—' His voice thickened as he broke off and kissed her parted lips hungrily. 'For the first time in my life I contemplated a meaningful relationship that was more than fleeting gratification. Imagine, then, my feelings when you declared that you only wanted me as a sex toy.'

'I didn't say that!' she protested, absolutely stunned by his revelations.

'As good as,' he insisted.

'I was trying to be what you wanted. I sort of half convinced myself that was what I wanted too—but then it got so hard. I had to throw your number away to stop myself ringing you.'

The confession made him laugh. Then, as the laughter died from his face, their eyes connected and his love was there for her to see. She shed the doubts and fears of the past weeks as though they had never been.

'The only time it ever mattered to me what a woman thought of my scars was with you, and you're the only woman who has kissed them, *cara.*'

Her lips quivered. 'I hate the idea of you hurting and me not being there.'

'You have healed me. I used to have flashbacks of the accident, but since the first time we made love there has been nothing.'

'Flashbacks!' She looked horrified. 'Did you go to therapy?'

'I didn't need therapy,' he scorned. 'I needed you.'

He bent his head to kiss her, and as much as Sam wanted to let him she knew there was something left to clear up. 'There's something I have to say, Alessandro. About Jonny. What I felt for him—it wasn't…real.' Lifting her eyes to his, she pressed a hand to her heart. 'What I feel for you—it's in here. It's real. I didn't know what love was until you taught me. You are my perfect lover, Alessandro, but I think you could be a perfect husband too, and a better than perfect father.'

He covered her hand with his. 'That is quite a title,' he said, his voice suspiciously husky. 'But,' he promised, 'I will try to live up to it every day of my life.'

Tears of joy stood out in her eyes as Sam's throat closed over with emotion. 'I thought you married me because of the baby,' she admitted.

'I was knocked sideways to hear about the baby,' he admitted quietly. 'And I am looking forward to being a father. But when I arrived at your flat that day I had this ring in my pocket.' He lifted her hand and touched the emerald that shone on her finger.

Sam's eyes widened. 'You were going to propose?' she whispered.

He nodded. 'And if I had got in my proposal before I learnt about the baby I think perhaps we would both have been saved some heartache... But that,' he said, 'is the past. We have the future to look forward to. Don't look now, but here comes Carlo with an umbrella, looking most disapproving. When we are alone he will scold me for letting you get wet. We should go indoors.'

Sam, her eyes shining with love, looked up at her tall, handsome husband and smiled. 'I'd go anywhere with you,' she told him, meaning it literally.

'When you look at me like that all I want to do is make love to you.'

'What's stopping you...?'

'Good point,' he said, scooping her up into his arms and carrying her, laughing, past a very startled-looking butler.

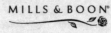

FREE

4 BOOKS AND A SURPRISE GIFT!

We would like to take this opportunity to thank you for reading this Mills & Boon® book by offering you the chance to take FOUR more specially selected titles from the Modern Romance™ series absolutely FREE! We're also making this offer to introduce you to the benefits of the Reader Service™—

- ★ **FREE home delivery**
- ★ **FREE gifts and competitions**
- ★ **FREE monthly Newsletter**
- ★ **Books available before they're in the shops**
- ★ **Exclusive Reader Service offers**

Accepting these FREE books and gift places you under no obligation to buy; you may cancel at any time, even after receiving your free shipment. Simply complete your details below and return the entire page to the address below. You don't even need a stamp!

YES! Please send me 4 free Modern Romance books and a surprise gift. I understand that unless you hear from me, I will receive 6 superb new titles every month for just £2.80 each, postage and packing free. I am under no obligation to purchase any books and may cancel my subscription at any time. The free books and gift will be mine to keep in any case.

P6ZEE

Ms/Mrs/Miss/Mr...Initials ....

BLOCK CAPITALS PLEASE

Surname ....

Address ....

....

....Postcode ....

Send this whole page to:
The Reader Service, FREEPOST CN81, Croydon, CR9 3WZ